Staben
Stabenow, Dana
Everything under the
    heavens

$13.95
ocn870546189
12/29/2014

# EVERYTHING
## UNDER THE
# HEAVENS

# Also by Dana Stabenow

# EVERYTHING
## UNDER THE
# HEAVENS

Book I *of* Silk and Song
by
### Dana Stabenow

Gere Donovan Press
Portland, Ore.

Gere Donovan Press
8825 SE 11th Avenue, Suite 210
Portland OR 97202
www.geredonovan.com

First Printing, 2014
ISBN 978-1-9366669-9-7

*This one is for*
*Barbara Peters,*
*who always believed.*

# Author's Note

There was no attempt to force my medieval characters to, in Josephine Tey's inimitable phrase, 'speak forsoothly.' When people spoke in 1320, they sounded as contemporary to each other as you and I do when we speak to each other today. I chose to offend neither the reader's eye nor my own oh-so-delicate writer's sensibilities with any *zounds!*-ing.

# Cast

**Agalia**. Jaufre's mother. Sold into slavery as "the Lycian Lotus."

**Anwar the Egyptian**. Slave dealer in Kashgar.

**Basil the Frank**. Wu Li's agent in Baghdad.

**Bo He**. Dai Fang's doorman.

**Chi Yuan**. Powerful Mandarin at the court of the Great Khan. Dai Yu's uncle.

**Chiang**. Edyk the Portuguese's manservant.

**Dai Fang**. Wu Li's second wife. Johanna's step-mother. Gokudo's lover.

**Dayir**. Aide to Bayan. Ogodei's father.

**Deshi the Scout**. Caravanmaster to Wu Li. Teaches Jaufre and Johanna soft boxing.

**Edyk the Portuguese**. Trader residing in Cambaluc.

**Eneas**. Wu Li's agent in Alexandria.

**Fatima**. Daughter of Malala and Ahmed, betrothed of Azar.

**Félicien**. A Frank from Dijon. Goliard, or student traveling the world. Has studied liberal arts in Paris and medicine in Salerno.

**Firas**. Nazari Ismaili from Alamut, the hereditary home of the Hashishin, or Assassins.

**Fakhir**. Wu Li's agent in Antioch.

**Farhad bin Mohammed**. Son of Sheik Mohammed of Talikan.

**Gokudo**. Samurai, expert in naginata (spear). Family killed and exiled from Cipangu in 1192. Dai Fang's lover and hatchet man.

**Grigori**. Wu Li's agent in Kabul.

**Hari**. Itinerant preacher, self-styled priest. "Sees" his destiny as to seek out new life and new religions.

**Hasan**. Wu Li's agent in Tabriz.

**Jaufre**. Orphaned on the Silk Road, rescued by Johanna's family, brought up as her brother, personal guard.

**Johanna**. Trader, singer, adventurer, thief. Daughter of Wu Li and Shu Ming, granddaughter of Marco Polo and Shu Lin.

**Madhar**. Wu Li's agent in Calicut.

**Mangu**. Cook in Wu Li's caravan.

**Niu Gang**. Wu Li's factotum.

**Ogodei**. Dayir's son, friend to Wu Li. A captain of the ten thousand risen to one of the twelve barons of the Shiang.

**Sheik Mohammed bin Assad of Talikan**. Father of Farhad.

**Shu Lin**. Shu Ming's mother, Marco Polo's concubine, the Khan's concubine and gift to Marco Polo, Johanna's grandmother.

**Shu Ming**. Johanna's mother, Wu Li's wife, Shu Lin's daughter, Marco Polo's daughter. Shu Shao's adopted elder sister.

**Shu Shao**. Also called "Shasha." Shu Ming's adopted younger sister. Nurse, friend, healer, wise woman.

**Wu Cheng**. Wu Li's brother. A eunuch, gelded by his parents for advancement at court. Fell out of favor when the old Khan died and, with the help of his brother, went into business as a trader on the Road.

**Wu Hai**. Marco's friend and Wu Li's father.

**Wu Li**. Johanna's father. Shu Ming's husband, and later Dai Fang's husband.

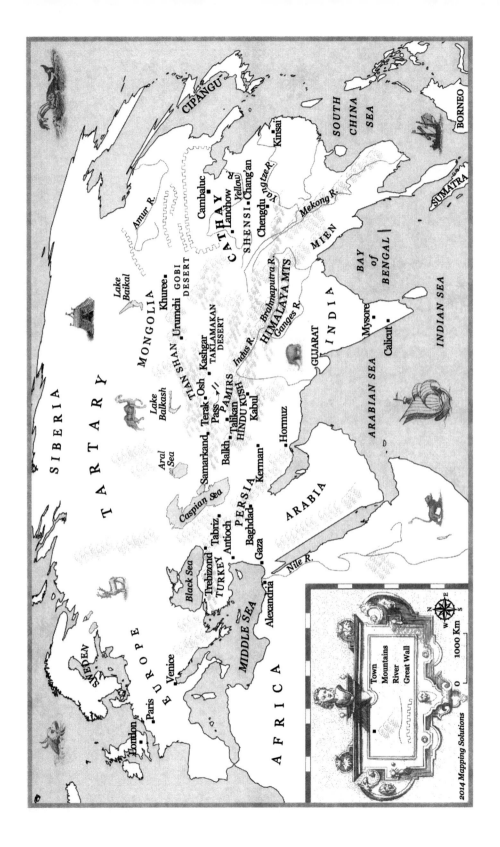

CIPANGU

BORNEO

SUMATRA

SOUTH
CHINA
SEA

Kinsai

Cambaluc

CATHAY

Lanchow
Yellow R.
Chang'an

Amur R.

SHENSI
Chengdu
Yangtze R.

MIEN

Mekong R.

BAY
of
BENGAL

INDIAN SEA

Lake
Baikal

MONGOLIA

Khuree

GOBI
DESERT

Urumchi

TIAN SHAN

TAKLAMAKAN
DESERT

Kashgar

Osh

Terak
Pass

PAMIRS

Talikan

HINDU KUSH

Kabul

Brahmaputra R.

HIMALAYA MTS

Indus R.

Ganges R.

GUJARAT

INDIA

Mysore

Calicut

ARABIAN SEA

SIBERIA

T A R T A R Y

Lake
Balkash

Aral
Sea

Samarkand

Balkh

Caspian Sea

PERSIA

Kerman

Hormuz

ARABIA

Black Sea

Trebizond

Antioch

Tabriz

Baghdad

TURKEY

Gaza

MIDDLE SEA

Alexandria

Nile R.

AFRICA

SWEDEN

Paris

London

Venice

EUROPE

Town
Mountains
River
Great Wall

N
W   E
S

1000 Km

0

# EVERYTHING
## UNDER THE
# HEAVENS

· Part I ·

# · One ·

1292 A.D.
*Cambaluc*

⊢————⊣

He was kept waiting not even an hour. As a mark of special favor, not lost on the others waiting on their own audiences in the cramped anteroom, Bayan's own personal aide came to escort him into the general's presence. They had travelled the Road together half a dozen times and Marco knew him well.

"Dayir!" They gripped each other's arms. "What's this I hear? A father, no less, and of a hearty son! Congratulations!"

Dayir, a short, muscular man near Marco's own age, had a wide, engaging grin. He gave his head a rueful shake. "Hearty is the word, I fear. He has a temper. My wife says he has his nurse terrorized."

Marco laughed. "He is a warrior already. What have you named him?"

"Ogodei."

"A good name, a strong name for the strong man to be."

"From your lips to the ears of all the gods, my friend."

Dayir opened a door and waved him forward, and Marco heard the door close gently behind him.

Bayan of the Hundred Eyes received him with courtesy and without ceremony, in a small, luxuriously appointed study. An exquisitely worked carpet in shades of red and gold covered the floor. Rolled maps, books and scrolls were slotted into shelves that reached the ceiling. A sliding door made of translucent rice paper was painted with bold bursts of golden chrysanthemums, and stood open to allow the intoxicating scent of the plum tree blossoms to drift inside.

"Hah, my Latin friend," Bayan said, rising from behind the lacquered table and reaching to pull Marco into a hearty embrace. "It has been too long."

"It has," Marco said, smiling. It was impossible to dislike Bayan when he greeted you so warmly and with such obvious good will.

"Sit, sit," Bayan said, waving him to a pillow-strewn couch. Tea and a tray of delicacies were brought by a female servant who teetered away again on bound feet. Kublai Khan's favorite general poured and served it himself. "Now, my Latin friend, tell me all about your recent journey on behalf of our most heavenly master. Where have you been? What have you seen?"

It was never the way of the East to come directly to the point, and it was only good manners that Marco pay for the privilege of this audience, so he obliged, over the next hour giving Bayan a vivid and detailed description of his journey to Cambay. Bayan listened with attention, asking many questions, and more than once rising to pull down a map from one of the shelves so Marco could trace out his route. Terrain, distance between stops, and the condition of the roads were Bayan's chief interests, after the amount and experience of armed troops, but Marco was also closely questioned as to the customs of local cultures, the goods for sale, and the beauty of the women in every region. It was a Cambaluc joke that Bayan's other nickname was Bayan of the Hundred Wives.

At last the general sat back and clapped his hands to order more tea. Again, he sent away the servant who brought it and poured it out with his own hands. "And you had no trouble along the way?" he said, offering Marco his cup.

"None. Oh, there was the usual pilfering, but no more than you might expect. We heard rumors of bandits in the hills outside of Bengal, and we saw one village that we were told was destroyed by them, but we never saw any ourselves." He smiled. "Carrying the Khan's paiza must be a guarantor of safe passage through the very bowels of hell itself, I think."

"How could it be otherwise?" Bayan said simply.

The eyes of the two men met. There was a long silence which Marco was determined not to break.

Bayan sighed. "I have spoken with our heavenly master, the Khan. He has said you may escort the Princess Kokachin to the court of King Arghun." A tart note entered into his voice. "He says it is to be hoped that you will succeed where those three nitwits of Arghun's failed."

Marco tried to conceal the leaping of his heart beneath a judicious expression. "To be fair, they couldn't know their chosen route home would lead through a civil war. It was simply bad luck."

"You make your own luck," Bayan said, who had certainly made enough of his own to be an authority. "At any rate, you, your father and your uncle will together be named the guardians of the Princess Kokachin. Your job is to deliver her safely to her bridegroom in the Levant."

"As always it is our very great joy to obey the wishes of the Son of Heaven," Marco said.

The promptness of this reply earned him a raised eyebrow. "As you say," Bayan said. "Your expedition will also be accompanied by delegations to the Pope in Rome, and to the kings of France, Spain, and England. You will be entrusted with messages to other leaders of Christendom as well."

"Expedition?" Marco said. "How large is this caravan going to be?"

"You will not be going overland, you will be going by sea," Bayan said, "in fourteen ships. The expedition is even now being assembled in Kinsai." He smiled to see Marco for once at such a loss for words. It didn't happen often.

"I am—humbled, as will be my father and my uncle, by the Great Khan's trust in us to lead such a grand mission." Marco knew a flood of happiness that at long last he would be going home, equalled only by the surge of satisfaction that it would be in such style. "When do we leave?"

"The court astrologers have decreed the last of the spring tides will be the most propitious day for your departure."

Marco cast an involuntary glance through the open door, where the garden was in full bloom.

"Yes, I know, my friend, we have left your departure a little late." Bayan leaned forward, a grave expression on his face, and dropped his voice to that barely above a whisper. "Within these four walls," he said, "I will tell you, my friend, that I do not know how much longer the Khan will live. His illness has progressed to where he rarely leaves his chambers. Very few are admitted into his presence." Bayan grimaced. "You'll know how bad it must be when I tell you that Chi Yuan sent for me, of all people, to visit our master the Great Khan in hopes I would ease his depression. A bit ironic, when we both know that Chi Yuan will be first in line with a dagger aimed at my heart when our master the Great Khan breathes his last."

Marco was silent. The struggle for power between the Mandarins and the Muslims at the court of Cambaluc was legendary. If Chi Yuan, a Mandarin and a jealous guard of the Great Khan's private life, had sent for Bayan of the Hundred Eyes, a Muslim, to relieve the Great Khan's spirits, they must be low indeed.

"He is leaving this life," Bayan said, his expression somber, "and he knows it. While he lives, you are safe here in Everything Under the Heavens. When he dies…"

The two men sat together in silence.

It was nothing Marco had not known before he had requested this audience. Many times over the past several years, ever since the Khan's health had begun to fail, the Polos had petitioned to leave the court and return home to Venice. Each time they had been refused, partly because the Great Khan feared what the loss of such effective tools would do to his own power and prestige, and partly because he was truly fond of them.

There was that much more urgency for his departure, that the Khan now lay dying. The twelve barons of the Shieng were jealous of his influence over their leader. While the Khan lived, their spite would be kept in check. When the Khan died…

"If we leave so soon, then I must return home at once," Marco said at last. "There is much to be done." His smile was rueful. "Shu Lin will be furious to be given so little time to pack."

Bayan did not smile back. "Alas…"

Marco stiffened. "There is a problem?"

Bayan placed his cup on the low table with exact precision, and delivered his next statement in a manner that showed that he knew just how unwelcome the words would be. "Our master the Great Khan has said that the beautiful Shu Lin and your equally lovely daughter, Shu Ming, must await your return here in Cambaluc."

"What!" Marco found himself on his feet without remembering how he got there.

Bayan smoothed the air with both palms. "Gently, my friend, gently. Sit. Sit."

After a tense moment Marco subsided to his pillows, his mind in turmoil. "But he gave her to me. She was a gift from the Great Khan, to me personally, Marco Polo, his most valued emissary. Or so he said." He could not quite keep the bitterness from his voice.

"Our master the Great Khan does not go back on his given word," Bayan said.

"But he holds my wife and my daughter hostage against my return!"

Again, Bayan smoothed the air. Again he said, "Gently, my friend, and lower your voice, I beg you. The eyes and ears of our master the Great Khan are everywhere, even here." He settled his hands on his knees and leaned forward again. "Commend Shu Lin and Shu Ming into the care of someone you trust. Escort the Princess Kokachin to her betrothed. When enough time has passed that our master the Great Khan's attention has turned elsewhere, I will send her to you."

"And if he dies in the meantime?"

"Gently, my friend, I beg you, gently. She is only a woman, and with you gone will have no status, and therefore offer no threat to anyone at court."

"She is safer with me gone, you mean."

"Yes." The soft syllable was implacable.

Marco sat in a leaden silence filled with despair.

Bayan leaned forward to put a hand on Marco's shoulder. "Think," he said, giving the other man a hard shake. "You must leave, you, your father and your uncle, for your own safety, for the sake of your very lives. Our master the Great Khan knows this as surely as do we ourselves, and he has found this way to make use of you for the last time. But you have been his friends for twenty years, and our master the Great Khan's heart aches at your parting. This is his way of ensuring himself that you come back to him."

Their eyes met. This was Marco's last departure from the court of the Great Khan, and both men knew it.

"How will I tell her?" Marco said heavily.

Bayan sat back. "Her father was one of the twelve barons of Shieng. She will understand."

She had. There were tears, but tears only of sorrow at their parting, and none of anger or remonstration. She did not blame him for his decision to leave his wife and daughter behind. Indeed, she said, as Bayan had, "If the Great Khan is as ill as Bayan says, it will be safer for us if you are gone when he dies." She had smiled up at him with wet but resolute eyes. "If Bayan says he will send us to you, then he will send us to you. We will be parted for only a short time. Have courage, my love."

That night in their bed he gathered into his arms and buried his face in her dark, fragrant hair. Here was wealth beyond measure, the highest status, unlimited privilege. Here was work he could do, and do well. Here was Shu Lin, beautiful and loving and loyal beyond words, and Shu Ming, three years old, as intelligent and healthy a child as any father could wish.

But here also was a once-strong and visionary ruler rendered timid and withdrawn by age, weary of spirit, limbs swollen with the gout that came from a diet of meat and sweets washed down with koumiss. He must leave, and he must leave soon. His father and his uncle were impatient to be away, and both of them had remonstrated with him over his reluctance to leave Shu Lin behind. The thought flashed through his mind that they would be glad not to have to explain her presence at Marco's side to their family in Venice.

"You have all the courage for both of us, it seems," he said.

Three-year-old Shu Ming was harder to convince, and his last sight of her was sobbing in her mother's arms. Wu Hai, Marco's partner in business and in many journeys over the years, stood at Wei Lin's side, square, solemn, solid. Wu Hai, one of the most successful businessmen from Cambaluc to Kinsai, was a man of worth and respectability. He had the added advantage of being well known to Shu Lin and Shu Ming.

"I give you my word," Wu Hai had said with a gravity befitting one undertaking a sacred oath, "your wife and your daughter will be no less in my house than members of my own blood."

Marco looked long upon the faces of his wife and child, and did not turn away until the firm hand of his uncle Maffeo pressed hard upon his shoulder.

The three Polos went out beneath the wooden arch that was the entrance of the only home Marco had known for the last twenty years. The sound of his daughter softly weeping followed him into the street.

He never saw wife, nor daughter, nor home again.

# · Two ·

1294 A.D.
*Cambaluc*

—

Kublai Khan died before Marco reached Venice, even before the Polos managed at last to deliver Princess Kokachin safely to her bridegroom. As the lady's consistently bad fortune would have it, he was also dead, murdered before ever she reached the kingdom of the Levant.

In Cambaluc, Kublai Khan's grandson, Temur, took the throne after months of uncertainty, followed by a struggle for power that did little to reinforce the stability of the Mongol realm. Trade went forward, of course, because nothing stopped trade, and Wu Hai returned from a trip to Kinsai shortly after Temur came to power.

Full of plans to open a new route to the pearl merchants of Cipangu, it was, shamefully, a full day before he noticed that Shu Lin and Shu Ming were missing. It took another day and making good on a threat to have his majordomo stripped to the waist and whipped before the assembled members of the family before he could discover where they were. He went straight to Bayan, the new emperor's chief minister.

By then, Shu Lin was dead.

Bayan did Wu Hai the courtesy of summoning him to his house to deliver the news in person. "Almost before the Great Khan breathed his last, the Mandarins and the Mongols were at each other's throats. Both factions were determined to remove any obstacles to their acquisition of power, as indeed was Temur Khan. Any favorites of the old Khan were suspect, and subject to immediate…removal."

"I understand," Wu Hai said, rigid with suppressed fury and guilt. "Marco, his father and his uncle were beyond their reach. His wife and child were not."

Bayan cleared his throat and dropped his eyes. "It may be that there was an informer who directed attention their way."

Wu Hai stood motionless, absorbing this. What Bayan was too tactful to say was that very probably someone in Wu Hai's own household had sold Shu Lin and Shu Ming in exchange for favor at the new court. His first wife had never liked Wu Hai's association with the foreign traders who brought him the goods he sold, that had made his fortune, that had provided the substantial roof over her head, the silks on her back and the dainties on her table.

"They were thrown into the cells below the palace," Bayan said. "From what I can discover, Shu Lin sold herself to the guards in exchange for Shu Ming's safety."

There was a brief, charged silence as both men remembered the delicate features and graceful form of the dead woman, and both flinched away from images of what she must have endured before her death.

There was shame in Bayan's face at his failure to protect his friend's wife and child. He had gravely underestimated the lengths to which desperate courtiers would go to curry favor with the new khan, and he admitted it now before a man who had also failed in his duty to a friend.

In a subdued voice, Wu Hai said, "And Shu Ming?"

Bayan's face lightened. "Alive. The doctors say she has suffered no harm. No physical harm." Bayan nodded at the open door of his study, and Wu Hai went through into the garden, where once again the plum trees were in bloom.

Shu Ming sat with her back to one of the trees, surrounded by fallen petals, a tiny figure in white silk embroidered with more plum blossoms. Of course, he thought, Bayan's people would have dressed her in mourning. He stopped some distance away, so that she would not be frightened.

It was unfortunate that she looked more like her father than her mother, long-limbed, hair an odd color somewhere between gold plate and turned earth, eyes an even odder color, somewhere between gray and blue, and, most condemning, round in shape, untilted, foldless. Her foreignness hit one like a blow, he thought ruefully. It would be all too easy to pick her out of any household in Everything Under the Heavens, and given the provincial and xenophobic nature of the native population, she would always be a target simply by virtue of breathing in and breathing out.

And now, her mother dead, her father gone beyond the horizon, she had no status in the community, no rights, no power. Her father had left them both well provided for, and Wu Hai had secured those funds, had, he thought bitterly, taken better care of their funds than he had of their persons. But money would not be not enough to buy her acceptance in Cambaluc.

The tiny figure had not moved, sitting cross-legged, her hands laying loosely in her lap, her eyes fixed on the middle distance. Her hair had been ruthlessly shorn, no doubt to rid her of the lice that infested every prison, and the cropped head made the slender stem of her neck look even more fragile rising up from the folds of her white tunic. There was almost no flesh remaining on her body. Her skin was translucent, her cheekbones prominent beneath it. Her tiny hands looked like paper over sticks.

He cleared his throat gently.

She turned her head to look at him, and he saw with a pang that she seemed somehow much older.

He bowed. "You see before you one Wu Hai, your father's most unworthy friend. Do you remember me?"

She inclined her head, her expression grave. "Of course I do, uncle," she said, giving him the correct honorific with the precisely correct emphasis and intonation. Again like her father, he thought, she had a facility for any language, her tongue adapting readily from Mongol to Mandarin.

"I am sorry I was away from home for so long," he said.

"My mother is dead, uncle," she said.

"To our loss and great sorrow," he said.

"And my father is gone."

"This, too, I know," he said.

"What will you do with her?" Bayan said before they left.

Wu Hai looked down at Shu Ming's tearstained face, asleep on his shoulder. "I have a son," he said.

"Ah," Bayan said, a thoughtful hand stroking his mustaches. "Have you given any thought to what your family will say?"

"I have no other family," Wu Hai said.

Bayan said no more.

Wu Hai returned to his home and turned everyone in the house into the street with what they had on their backs, wife and servants all, with the sole exception of his son.

His wife sobbed and groveled at his feet. "Where will I go, husband? What will I do?"

Before them all he deliberately put the sole of his foot against her shoulder and shoved her through the gate. She rolled and rose to her feet, the lacquer on her face running in great rowels down her cheeks. "You had a wife!" Her voice rose to a scream. "What need had you of another!"

"She had a husband," Wu Hai said. He surveyed the throng of people gathered around her. Not one of them could meet his eyes. He remembered the delicate features and the gentle disposition of his friend's wife, brutalized and despoiled and then destroyed, from nothing more than petty jealousy.

"I have no wife," he said, raising his own voice so that it would be heard over the sobs and wails of the people who had once formed his household. So they would understand fully the price of betrayal, he himself closed the heavy wooden doors in their faces. The bar dropped inexorably into its brackets with a loud and final thud.

He turned to face his son.

Wu Li was a sturdy and handsome fellow, standing with his legs braced and his thumbs in his belt in imitation of his father. He met Wu Hai's eyes squarely, although his face was a little pale.

"Do you understand what happened here, my son?" Wu Hai said.

The boy hesitated, and then nodded once, firmly. "I do, father."

"What, then?"

Unflinching, the boy said steadily, "There is no excuse for betraying a guest in one's home."

Wu Hai's wife had been an unaffectionate and inattentive mother. He nodded. "It is well," he said.

He sold the house for an extortionate price to one of Temur's new-minted nobles and built a new home on property he owned outside of the city. It sat on the banks of the Yalu, and he built a dock and warehouses there as well, which, once Temur's policies allowed the realm to recover from the economic instability caused by the ruinous wars of his grandfather, proved to be a profitable move.

The first ceremony conducted beneath the roof of the new house was the marriage of his son, Wu Li, 9, to Shu Ming, 5. The marriage was in name only until both children had come of age, but in the interim it gave Shu Ming rank and citizenship, entitled to all the rights and at least the outward respect of the citizens of Everything Under the Heavens.

Temur was an enlightened ruler who appointed people to positions of responsibility regardless of their ethnicity or religion. At court Mongols worked beside Han Chinese, Muslims, Confucians and even a few Latins, usually priests who were missionaries for their faiths, but some merchants as well. In this he was truly the grandson of Kublai Khan. But Wu Hai, who until the end of his life held himself responsible for the betrayal and death of Shu Lin, wasn't taking any chances with the life of her daughter. He ignored the whispers in the Chinese community, the covert looks his family received when abroad, even the mutterings of his own parents.

He was every bit as honorable a man as Marco had believed him to be when he committed his wife and daughter into Wu Hai's care.

# · Three ·

1312 A.D.
*Five days from Kashgar*

⊢——⊣

Johanna had graduated to her own camel.

Her father, Wu Li, had told her that if she managed to keep her seat from the beginning of Kuche to the city of Kashgar that he would let her off the leading string for the journey home. Shu Ming's protest had died on her lips when she met Wu Li's indulgent glance.

Johanna's camel was young and small, but what she lacked in size and maturity she made up for in energy and a fierce determination to be out in front. At Johanna's nudge she lengthened her stride to something approaching a canter.

"Johanna," Wu Li said in a warning voice.

"I'm sorry, father," Johanna said, with an impish glance over her shoulder. "She wants to run."

"Wu Li," Shu Ming said, and he looked at her with an expression warring between guilt and pride.

He shrugged, a twinkle in his eye. "She wants to run."

Shu Ming looked at the receding figure of their daughter. "They both want to run," she said.

By now three lengths ahead of Deshi the Scout, Johanna was concentrating so hard on keeping her balance while at the same time keeping her back straight that she didn't see the body until her camel stumbled over it. Her only consolation was that Deshi had not seen it, either, although to be fair the rest of the remnants of the other caravan were well buried in the shifting desert sand. Johanna was almost thrown, almost but luckily not quite.

Nevertheless, Wu Li had seen. He kicked his camel into a trot and arrived at her side at the same time as Deshi the Scout. "All right, daughter?"

All three of them stared at the desiccated limb that her mount's hoof had exposed.

Johanna swallowed. "All right, father."

"Good. Stay in your saddle."

Her back straightened and her chin rose. "Of course, father."

Shu Ming had seen, too, and came up fast, and when she yanked on the reins her camel stopped so abruptly that its hindquarters slid out from beneath it and rider and camel both skated past on the sand. On any other day the sight would have provoked laughter and teasing. Today Johanna managed only a shaken smile.

Deshi the Scout already had his bow out and an arrow nocked, his face stern as he scanned the horizon. Wu Li pulled his mount around and raised a hand. The line of camels halted, some expressing their displeasure by groaning and spitting. One kicked out with his right hind leg, narrowly missing Mangu the Cook, who let loose with a string of cheerful curses that died on his lips when he looked ahead to see what the problem was.

Wu Li kicked his camel into a kneeling position and slid down, loosening his knife as he went, but the bodies were days dead and the only sound on this lonely expanse of undulating dunes was the rasp of wind on sand. He looked at Deshi the Scout, who withdrew to the nearest rise, there to keep a watch in every direction at once.

By the time they had uncovered the bodies of three camels, a horse, and thirteen people, it was almost sunset. Wu Li sent a rider ahead to Kashgar to alert the authorities and to let Shu Shao know they would be late in arriving. Mangu located a small oasis with an even smaller spring and two frail date palms half a league from the road and supervised the setting up of a camp while Wu Li gathered what evidence he could to reconstruct what had happened.

Deshi the Scout found a scrap of sheer red fabric. The edge was hemmed with gilt spangles. "Gujarat weave," he said.

"There are no women or children among the bodies," Wu Li said. "Muslim bandits, then. Every year they move further east. Remember the Buddhist shrine we found last year?"

"What was left of it I do." Deshi the Scout hawked and spat. "This kind of thing didn't happen when the old Khan was alive."

Wu Li agreed, but silently, as even here, a thousand leagues from the capitol, one could never be sure who was listening. Kublai Khan's heirs had been competent but they were not visionaries, and they had allowed the politics of court and the luxuries of the throne to distract their attention from the disintegrating infrastructure of their empire. Over the years the Road had become slowly but steadily more perilous.

They ate without appetite and mostly in silence that evening, and turned in early. Wu Li took the first watch, knife at his side, bow at his knee.

They had not pitched the yurts in case they had to to move suddenly and quickly. For a long time into that very long night Johanna watched the figure of her father, back to the coals of the fire, the fronds of the two palms hanging limp and listless over his head, a black sky glittering with stars above.

Johanna woke to meet the alert eyes of Deshi the Scout. The rising sun set fire to the endless eastern horizon and illuminated his grave smile. She crept from beneath the blankets she shared with Wu Li and Shu Ming and retired behind a convenient dune to attend to the call of nature.

She squatted, holding her trousers out of the way. The stream of urine steamed in the cold morning air, the acrid smell striking her nostrils. She was almost finished when the sand directly beneath her feet heaved up. She screamed and tumbled backwards, head over heels. She scrambled to her feet, hauling at her trousers.

Her scream had a particularly piercing and far-reaching quality, and behind her she heard startled voices and loud oaths. "Johanna! Where is Johanna?" her mother cried.

Before her astonished gaze the sand rose up and assumed a human shape. For a wild moment she thought a demon was materializing before her eyes, an apparition out of one of Deshi's tales that would pull her back beneath the sand with him, there to devour her whole. She screamed again, backing away, tripping over her own feet and falling once more.

The sand cascaded in sheets from the apparition. As Wu Li and Shu Ming hurtled around the dune on one side and Deshi the Scout came around it from the other, weapons drawn and ready for action, the figured was revealed to be a boy hardly older than Johanna herself.

He was thin to the point of emaciation, his blue eyes red-rimmed, his hair stiff with sand, his skin peeling from sunburn. He wore only a filthy kilt that might once have been white in color, and leather sandals.

His only possession was a sword as tall as he was. A luminous steel blade rising from a heavy hilt encrusted with stones. As Wu Li and Deshi approached he raised the blade high, or tried to, the muscles of his scrawny arms bunched with effort. He actually got it up over his head, staggering a little, before the weight of all that metal got the better of him and his arms trembled and gave way. The sword dropped behind him, point down in the sand, his hands still grasping the hilt.

Tears made runnels in the dirt caked on his cheeks, but he didn't seem afraid. On the contrary, he was swearing like Mangu the Cook when the millet burned to the bottom of the pot. "I'll kill you!" he said. He was trying to shout but his voice came out in a hoarse croak. "Don't you touch me, or I'll kill you all!"

Wu Li and Deshi the Scout, who had halted, exchanged a glance. The boy had spoken in Aramaic.

Wu Li turned back to the boy and spoke in the same language. "Gently," he said. "We mean you no harm."

The boy wiped his face on his shoulder, leaving both smeared with dirt and tears and snot, a fearful sight. "I'll kill you all," he said, but the fierceness had drained out of him. His head drooped as if it was suddenly too heavy for his neck.

Johanna, yanking the drawstring of her pants tight, was red-faced and furious, embarrassed at being frightened by a boy no older or bigger than she was. She opened her mouth to call him every name she could think of, and after a life spent on the road with her father, her supply was endless. She encountered her father's eye, and shut her mouth again.

"My name is Wu Li," said her father. "I am a merchant of Cambaluc, traveling to Kashgar." He gestured. "We have food. Grant us the honor of sharing it with you."

Perhaps it was the formality of his speech, or perhaps it was the manner in which he made it, man to man. The boy's shoulders straightened, and when Wu Li turned and walked back to their camp he followed, the tip of the sword leaving a thin line in the sand behind him.

Mangu brought him a meal of dried dates and fresh baked naan and the boy tore into it with ferocious greed and looked around for more. "Gently, my friend," Wu Li said, "gently. You have been hungry too long to eat too much all at once." He handed the boy a skin full of water. "Drink now, small swallows. Let your stomach remember how to digest its food."

The rest of the company served themselves. The warm bread and the hot black tea took the edge off their hunger and the rising sun burned the chill from the morning air.

"What is your name?" Wu Li said.

The boy blinked. "Jaufre," he said at last, as if only just remembering it himself.

"And how do you come to be here, Jaufre?"

The boy looked at the steam rising from the thick earthenware cup. "My father was a guard on a caravan traveling from Baghdad to Karakorum."

Wu Li looked at the sword laying at the boy's side. "That is his sword?"

A grubby hand touched the hilt for reassurance. "Yes."

"I see."

As did they all. Even beneath all the grime, it was obvious the sword was made of the finest steel, probably Damascus steel, Wu Li thought, and he suspected that the stones in the hilt might be genuine gemstones. A valuable asset, indicating either the wealth of its owner or great favor on the part of the patron who had bestowed it. It was doubtful that a caravan guard could ever afford to buy one such for himself.

That Jaufre had it now meant that his father was dead, because such a weapon would not have left his possession any other way. Wu Li only wondered how the boy had taken it without the raiders noticing.

He said, "And you traveled with your father?"

"Yes." The boy's face twisted. "And my mother."

Behind her Johanna heard Shu Ming draw in a breath.

"You were attacked," Wu Li said. It wasn't a question.

"Yes."

"By whom?"

"Many men. On horses."

"Horses? Not steppe ponies?"

"No. Horses."

Not Mongols then, Wu Li thought. "How were the men dressed?"

The boy looked confused but answered readily. "Mintans and trousers."

"On their heads?"

"Sariks."

"With their faces covered?"

The boy nodded.

"Beda," Deshi the Scout said.

"Or Turgesh," Wu Li said. "Although I've never heard of either of them this far east before." He turned back to the boy and spoke again, keeping his voice matter of fact. "Your father?"

The boy's chin trembled and then firmed. "I buried him."

"How did they not see you?" Wu Li indicated the sword with his chin. "Or the sword?"

"He fell on me, to hide me from them." The boy drew in a shaky breath, and Wu Li could only imagine how the moments had passed for the boy, held motionless beneath the dying weight of his father. "And then before they could search him the wind came and blew the sand. I let it cover me." He swallowed and looked away. "Us. I think I must have fallen asleep."

Lost consciousness, more like, Wu Li thought.

"When the storm stopped, I woke up and they were gone. So," the boy said drearily, "I buried him, and I took his sword, and I walked until I found water."

Shu Ming made a soft sound of distress, and Wu Li knew she was picturing in her mind the small, desolate figure alone on the trackless yellow sands, beneath the scorch of an unforgiving sun. "How did you find water?"

"There were birds," the boy said. "I followed them."

"Lucky," Deshi said in Mandarin.

Smart, Wu Li thought. "And your mother?" he said.

The boy's face contorted with the effort not to cry. "They took her. They took all the women. And the camels and the horses that weren't killed in the fighting." His head drooped. "I looked for tracks, but the wind blew them all away."

Wu Li raised his head and met Shu Ming's eyes. "How long ago was that?"

The boy squinted at the rising sun. "Eight days? Nine?" He shook his head, exhaustion showing plainly on his face. "I buried myself in the sand every night to keep warm, and again every day when the sun got too hot to bear."

"You did well," Wu Li said.

The boy's head jerked up. "I hid," he said with bitter emphasis.

"And you're alive," Wu Li said.

The boy stared at him. "I didn't even try to fight them."

"You're alive," Wu Li said again. "What made you show yourself this morning?"

The boy reddened and he glared at Johanna. "She peed on me!"

Johanna, who had been rapt with interest at the tale thus far, went red again in her own turn. "I didn't know you were there!"

Everyone burst into laughter, except for the two combatants. Wu Li recovered first, and said mildly, "Well, Jaufre, we will be glad to offer you safe passage to Kashgar, if that is your wish." Again he gave the illusion of Jaufre having a choice, and Jaufre, who was old enough to know better, was grateful for this sparing of his dignity, even if he was too young to put a name to it.

Wu Li looked up at the circle of faces. "Finish your breakfasts, water the camels and fill the water skins. We move on as soon as we strike camp."

He didn't say what he was thinking, what they were all thinking. With Persian bandits marauding this far east, the sooner they were behind caravanserai walls, the better.

They were away in half an hour, the boy Jaufre in the saddle behind Johanna, the sword strapped to the saddlebag behind him. It was difficult to remain aloof in such close proximity. He smelled, but it wouldn't have been polite to say so and besides, it wasn't his fault. After a while she said in a stiff little voice, "My name is Johanna."

She'd given up hope of a response to her overture when he said, "Johanna. Johanna? There was a queen named Johanna once. Or so my father told me."

"Really?"

"She was the sister of a great warrior king named Richard the Lionheart," Jaufre said. His voice was dull, but he seemed determined to pay his passage on the back of her camel with the full story. "They were from my father's country, an island far to the west. She was sent to marry the king of another island. And then he died, and she was held hostage, and her brother had to rescue her."

"And then what happened?"

"I don't remember all of it. She was shipwrecked on the way home and her brother had to rescue her again, and then she almost married two other kings, and then she did marry a count of the Franks, and led his army while he was away."

"And then what?"

"I think she became a nun."

"What's a nun?"

Jaufre seemed to wake up a little at this question. "You don't know what a nun is?"

"No. What is it?"

"Well, it's—she is like a monk, only she's a woman."

"Oh." All the monks Johanna had met were Buddhists, and male. It was hard to imagine a woman dressed in a skimpy orange robe and bare feet whose only possession was a wooden bowl used for both eating and begging. She wondered if the other Johanna had had to shave her head, like the monks did, and if so, what kept her crown on afterward.

They rode in silence after that. From time to time during that first long day, as the road passed swiftly beneath, she would seek out the familiar, reassuring figures of her mother and her father.

To have lost one was unthinkable. To lose both? Unendurable.

"You will stay with us," she said to the horizon of undulating sand, to the bleached blue of the sky overhead, to the rump of Deshi's camel. She was staking a claim.

Jaufre, drained from his ordeal and hypnotized by the rhythm of the camel's swaying gait, had fallen asleep with his head on her shoulder, drooling a little from the corner of his mouth.

"You will stay with us," she said again, more softly this time, but with even more conviction.

He snored, too.

# · Four ·

⊢——⊣

There were no stories or singing around the fire that night or
any other between there and Kashgar. They reached the city in
three days instead of five, pushing their mounts hard, making
dry camps with everyone taking turns on watch during the night, arms
to hand, even Johanna and her small bow, no one getting much sleep.
Johanna saw the relief on her father's face when the high walls of the city
came into view.

They halted in the yard of the large caravansary that sat just outside
the city walls. Dusty camels knelt, bawling out their hunger and ostlers
moved in a continual dance to remain just out of reach of their snapping
yellow teeth.

A young woman approached, neat in clean robes correctly tied, and
bowed. "It is good to see you safely arrived, Master Wu." She bowed to
Shu Ming. "Sister."

"It is good to have arrived safely, Shasha," Wu Li said with a certain
grimness. "Your own journey?"

"Without incident, master. Niu Gang and I made excellent time."
Her tone and expression were bland but her eyes were sharp as they
scanned the rest of the party, noting the addition of Jaufre perched
behind Johanna with interest but no surprise. "I have secured rooms for
our party and hired staff for our stay. Niu Gang is arranging feed for the
camels with the stable master. Six merchants, including the venerable
Wen Yan, have requested first looks at our goods, and the magistrate
requests an appointment at your earliest convenience."

Wu's expression eased and he gave her a formal bow. "As always, Shu Shao, you reward my trust tenfold."

She bent her head without embarrassment and without arrogance, accepting the compliment as no more or less her due. Jaufre, looking on, thought that she wore the assurance of a woman many years her senior. Johanna, too, seemed to him much older than her six.

But then Jaufre, though he did not realize it then, felt like an old man himself. A life lived on the Road encouraged the early acquisition of skills of all kinds. You either survived it or you did not. If you did, you matured fast.

Wu Li busied himself with supervising the unloading of the bolts of silk and bales of tea and crates of porcelain. Shu Shao led Shu Ming and Johanna to their rooms. They were on the second floor, in a corner. Shu Ming opened the shutters of two windows that looked out over a garden with a blue-tiled fountain tinkling in the middle of it.

"Very nice," Shu Ming said. "How much are we paying?"

"No more than we can afford."

The two women smiled at each other.

Their hair was drawn severely back into identical thick braids, but there any similarity ended. Shu Ming was taller, her hair a tawny mass with gold glints, her eyes a golden brown. Shu Shao's hair was smooth and black, her face a round-cheeked oval of olive skin, with tilted eyes as dark as her hair. Shu Ming moved with unconscious grace, her eyelashes casting long shadows on her cheeks. Shu Shao moved with economy and purpose, and her gaze was direct, alert and missed nothing. Shu Ming smelled of peonies in full bloom. Shu Shao smelled of peonies, too, and of ginger and ginseng and licorice and cinnamon. Shu Shao was nearer in age to Johanna but her assurance and self-possession made her seem older than both of them.

"Mother?"

Shu Ming turned to smooth back a curl that had escaped from Johanna's fat bronze braid. "What is it, my love?"

Johanna raised serious eyes to her mother's. "I think Jaufre should stay with us."

The hand stilled.

"Jaufre is the boy?" Shu Shao said.

Shu Ming nodded. "And why is that exactly?" she said to Johanna.

Johanna was only six, and the complexities of human emotion were as yet beyond her articulation. "Because we found him," she said. "Because he belongs to us."

"He belongs to himself, Johanna," Shu Ming said, but her voice was gentle.

"He doesn't have anyone else, mother." Eyes a shade darker than her own were openly pleading. "There is no one he knows here in Kashgar, and no family or home waiting for him in Baghdad. There is only us."

Shu Ming was silent for a moment.

It was a great grief to her that thus far Johanna had been the only child she had been able to carry to term, and her only child to have survived birth. Married to Wu Li almost before she could remember as a matter of survival, it was her very great fortune to have been joined to someone who loved her and cared for her enough to take her with him on his journeys, to have not taken, at least not yet, another wife or concubine. He had never betrayed by word or deed his wish for more children, for a son to inherit his father's business, to carry his father's line forward into immortality, to honor his father's and his father's bones. She looked into Johanna's eyes, and she feared what the future had in store for her daughter. A woman alone, without family, was in peril by her very existence on the earth.

She thought of Jaufre, that fierce young boy who had been ready to take on Wu Li and Deshi the Scout and their entire caravan in defense of himself and his father's sword.

Young as she had been, Shu Ming never forgot the days and weeks she had spent in the cells below the palace in Cambaluc, of the things she had seen, of the things her mother had done for a drop of water or a grain of rice. She alone in Wu Li's entourage truly understood the repressed horror that dulled Jaufre's eyes.

Given his ordeal, there would have been no reproaches if all he had done was eat and sleep and ride over the past three days, but instead he had contributed to the daily work of the caravan with ability and determination. He knew as well as Johanna the knots required to secure a pack on a camel's back and he didn't balk at joining her in collecting dried dung from the Road for that night's campfire. Shu Ming had spared a bit of water to clean off the worst of the dirt and had cobbled together a change of clothing, so his appearance was much improved. She liked both the erectness of his spine and the directness of his gaze, and found him well-spoken when addressed.

He also looked a lot more like her daughter than almost anyone else they knew back in Cambaluc, with the exception of those foreign merchants and priests who always clustered about the royal court, seeking attention and favor.

She reminded herself that he was scarcely older than her daughter, and smiled at Johanna. "Let us see what your father says."

Johanna smiled. She knew what that meant, and she danced away to tell Jaufre he was coming home with them.

His brow knotted. "I can't come with you, Johanna," he said.

"Why not?" she said, dismayed.

"I have to find my mother," he said.

When called before Wu Li that evening after dinner, he repeated himself. "I have to find my mother."

Wu Li looked at the small, militant figure planted in front of him, and knew respect, even an odd sense of pride in this foundling. Still, he could not allow the boy to go haring off into the blue. Chances were he would only end up in a slave market, too. But it would be much better if the boy came to that realization on his own. "Do you know where she has been taken?"

The boy hesitated, and then gave his head a reluctant shake.

"Do you have a plan as to where to begin to look?"

A longer pause. Another shake of the head.

Wu Li sat back, scratching his chin in a thoughtful manner. "I see. Well, I can put some inquiries to people I know here in Kashgar. We will need a description. Did you look like her?"

"No. She had dark hair and eyes. I look like my father." The firm chin gave just a suspicion of a quiver before his face resumed its determined cast.

"Was she Persian?"

"Greek," the boy said. "My father was from Britannia."

"A Crusader?" Wu Li said. Or the son of one, perhaps, as the last Christian outpost in the Levant had fallen to the Mamluks over twenty years before.

"A Templar."

"Ah." A lapsed one, then, as Templars were supposed to be celibate.

It happened. Wu Li's agent in Antioch was a former Templar who had renounced Christianity for Islam and embraced the notion of multiple wives and unlimited concubines with tireless enthusiasm. "About your mother," he said. "The slave market in Kashgar is the largest between here and Kabul. It is possible she and the others captured from your caravan will be brought here to be sold." He reflected briefly on how much such a sale might bring. Generally speaking, a woman who had had a child would not fetch the highest price, which was reserved for virgins. But Jaufre was a handsome lad and had probably had equally handsome parents. Wu Li could only hope that if his mother was found that the price would not be beyond the reach of his purse, as he well knew that he would be expected to meet it by wife and daughter both. "What is your mother's name?"

"Agalia," the boy said. "It means joy in Greek."

"Pretty," Wu Li said, keeping his inevitable reflections to himself.

The boy left, step light with hope.

"Do you really think it is possible we may find her here?" Shu Ming said later.

Wu Li shrugged. "It is possible. But not likely. And we must be very careful. Slavery is not illegal in Kashgar."

She was combing her damp hair with the intricately carved sandalwood comb he had brought her from Mysore the year Johanna was born, the only year she had not traveled with him. Yet again he was conscious of the gratitude due his father, who had chosen so well for his son's bride. The condemning looks that her obvious foreign blood drew in Cambaluc, the shunning by the Chinese community there, it was all worth it for a life spent with a woman like this at his side. Beautiful, intelligent, adventurous. What more could one want in a mate?

And they weren't in Cambaluc now. He stretched out on the bed and put his hands behind his back to watch her as she bent over, her hair hanging almost to the floor, and began with short, patient strokes to disentangle first the very ends of the thick mane, working slowly up to her scalp. When she was finished she stood up straight and tossed her hair back, where it fell in a flyaway cloud of shining brown curls, with the most intriguing streaks of gold and bronze and cinnamon. She was flushed and smiling, having felt his eyes on her all the while, knowing how much he enjoyed watching her at this particular task.

The first night at their destination was always a special night, no matter how tired or travel-worn they were. The first night was a celebration of the return of privacy after weeks and sometimes months spent sleeping in tents in the open or in caravansary rooms shared with ten others. The ritual included bathing, clean clothes, a meal of local delicacies they could eat sitting on clean mats, a long, delicious night in a clean, comfortable bed, and no need to set a guard or to rise too early the following morning.

She was wrapped in the Robe of a Thousand Larks, a garment of gold silk elaborately embroidered in silk thread with the brilliant colors of many larks in many attitudes, yellow throats arched, plump orange chests puffed out, black and yellow banded wings spread in flight, green heads cocked to one side, red beaks open in song. Bordered with brilliant flowers and green leaves and black branches, bound closely to the waist with a matching sash, it seemed to Wu Li that the robe made all the light in the world gather in this one room solely to illuminate Shu Ming's slender, elegant figure.

And it made his hands itch to loosen the knot of that sash.

She set the comb carefully to one side and walked to him, and the whereabouts of Jaufre's mother and indeed everything else were forgotten for the rest of the evening.

The next morning he presented himself at the magistrate's office as requested and saw with pleasure and not a little relief that the magistrate was not alone. "Ogodei!"

He stepped forward and the two men exchanged a hearty embrace. From a corner of his eye he took note of the magistrate's visible relaxation, and he hid a smile. Having a captain of a Mongol ten thousand in one's backyard was never a cause for joy unconfined.

"Wu Li, my good friend." A man of ability, vigor and stamina, the Mongol chief was dressed in soldier's robes, his long black mustaches rivaling Bayan's own. He looked fit and bronzed from long days spent in the saddle, patrolling the western borders of the Khan's vast empire. "I find you, as always, far from home."

Wu Li laughed. "The last time was, when? Khuree, at the summer court, at the ceremony of the gifts?"

"Worse!" Ogodei covered his eyes and gave a dramatic shudder. "In Kinsai last fall. You had just returned from Cipangu, that far and obstinate country, laden with fine pearls and full of plans as to where and to whom to sell them." He laughed, throwing back his head. "As I recall, you sold some to me."

"But then," Wu Li said, a glint in his eye and a manifestly false tone of apology in his voice, "there are so many likely recipients for them."

This time Ogodei's crack of laughter was so loud it made the magistrate jump, although for the sake of his dignity he did his best to conceal it. "True enough, Wu Li, my old friend. I am rich in wives and in concubines." He cocked an eyebrow. "And the beautiful Shu Ming?"

"Flourishing."

"And your daughter?"

"Healthy, shooting up like a weed in springtime." Wu Li exchanged a bow with the magistrate. "What brings you to the edge of the world, O great captain of the Khan?"

The three men settled into chairs and leaned forward to discuss the state of their mutual world.

Later, Wu Li gave Shu Ming the gist of it. "Jaufre's caravan was not the only one attacked this season. Reports have been coming in from as far as Kabul, and even beyond. The Persian tribes are becoming ever more bold in their incursions. The Khan has placed several of his ten thousands to patrol the Road this season and deal with any trouble."

"He's missed some," Shu Ming said.

He shot her a warning glance. It took only one informer to turn criticism to treason.

"You will still look for Jaufre's mother?" Shu Ming said.

"I gave the boy my word," Wu Li said, and Shu Ming said no more.

Wu Li was as good as his word. He had been closely questioned by Ogodei and the magistrate on the remains of Jaufre's caravan, and had used the interview to pose cautious questions of his own. He omitted any mention of Jaufre, and he had laid the most strict prohibition on all his people from making any public reference as to how the boy had come to be among them. Since Kashgar was the nearest available market for stolen goods, it stood to reason someone affiliated with the thieves would be in the city, very much alive to the news of an eyewitness and bound to pass it on. Ogodei was a vigorous and capable captain and Wu Li had no doubt his progress up the ranks would be steady and possibly even legendary, but even he could not guarantee the safety of one small boy in a city the size and duplicity of Kashgar. Anonymity was a much more sensible solution.

Wu Li bought a cap for the boy to cover hair that, when washed, proved to be the color of gold, a distinctive, memorable and in these parts unusual shade, and told him to wear it every moment he was outside their rooms in the caravansary.

Over the next week as Wu Li met with his agent in Kashgar, his fellow merchants and prospective buyers, he let fall the judicious word here and there that he was looking for a Greek woman answering to the name of Agalia. A free woman, recently widowed, who might through a series of unfortunate circumstances have had the additional misfortune of falling prey to slavers. He wasn't asking for himself, but family in Antioch had contacted Basil the Frank, his agent in Baghdad, and as a favor to Basil… Yes, yes, of course, the utmost discretion…

The Honorable Wu Li of Cambaluc, following in the footsteps of his father, the Honorable Wu Hai, had taken great care over many visits to maintain good relations with the city of Kashgar, paying into the city's treasury with every appearance of good will his tithe of monies earned through sales of his goods. He had even taken on a local orphanage as a personal concern, in donations of cash, food and goods. Neither was he a stranger to the local mosque, Buddhist monastery, or Nestorian church. He had no intention of embarrassing any good citizen of Kashgar for legally acquiring property in the form of a slave. But if such a slave had been purchased, it was just possible that she could be sold again, immediately, and at a modest profit. The Honorable Wu Li would be very grateful, and as every citizen of Kashgar knew, such gratitude had a way of manifesting itself in very real terms, if not immediately then at some time in the future. The citizens of Kashgar, traders to the bone, took always the long view.

In the meantime, Jaufre and Johanna, shadowed at a discreet distance by Deshi the Scout, sallied forth into the great bazaar, where a surgeon pulled a rotten molar from the mouth of a groaning patient with his wailing wife at his side. Next to the surgeon's shop a blacksmith replaced a cast shoe on a braying donkey. Another stall featured an endless array of brilliant silks, presided over by a black-veiled woman who, when the imam issued the call to prayer, excused herself from her customers, produced a small rug, and knelt to prostrate herself toward the east.

There were tents filled with nothing but soaps, powders to clean one's hair, picks to clean one's fingernails, pumice to smooth one's callouses, creams and lotions to soften one's skin, perfumes to make one irresistible to the opposite sex. There was cotton by the bale and by the ell, and tailors to make it up into any garment one wished. Carpenters made chair legs and rolling pins and carts. Herbalists made up mixtures of spices to season lamb, ease a head cold, hasten a birth. A tinsmith cut rolled sheets of tin into pieces for buckets, tubs, pots and pans. An ironworker fashioned chisels and hammers. Potters sat behind rows of bowls, pitchers and urns glazed in golden brown and cool green.

One huge tent was filled with coarse sacks with the tops open and the sides partly rolled down to display a vast selection of dried fruits and nuts, apricots from Armenia, olives from Iberia, almonds and dates from Jordan, pistachios from Balkh. There were carts piled high with sheep's lungs dyed pink and green and yellow and stuffed with spiced meats and cooked grains. One sweating man rendered a pile of pomegranates as tall as he was into cups of cool, tart, ruby-red juice, unperturbed by the dozens of wasps and flies buzzing around him. "Hah, daughter of the honorable Wu Li! You have returned to Kashgar!"

Johanna beamed at him. "Well met, Ahmed! Yes, we have returned, and we are here to trade."

He refilled their cups without charge, trading Kashgar gossip for the gossip of the Road, and Jaufre was impressed by Johanna's knowledge and confidence, and the ease with which she slipped from Mandarin, the language spoken among members of the caravan, and Persian, the lingua franca of Kashgar. He was even more impressed by the respect Ahmed accorded Johanna, and the gravity with which he listened to her replies to his questions. Fifty years Ahmed's junior, she barely came up to his waist, and yet he attended her conversation with a serious frown that didn't look as if he were indulging a child.

Next to Ahmed's stall green-glazed earthenware jars of olive oil, big enough to hold both Johanna and Jaufre with room to spare, were stacked against bales of hay. The vendor had set up a crude wooden table with a bowl of the oil available for tasting. Placed conveniently next door was a naan stall. A woman in a colorful scarf tied low on her forehead, her sleeves turned back to her elbows, was kneading a mass of dough in a large open bowl. Her husband presided over the oven, a tall earthenware pot larger than the oil urns, buried in glowing coals. He tore off chunks of dough to pat them into rounds and slap them against the inside surface of the pot. When that side had browned he peeled them off and slapped them down again on the other, uncooked side. The smell of baking bread made Johanna's stomach growl and the baker's wife smile. She gave them two rounds each, saying with a twinkle, "Still the finest bread in all of Kashgar, yes, young miss?"

"Oh, yes, thank you, Malala! Is Fatima here?"

"She is, young miss," Malala said. "She is on an errand for me at present, but doubtless you will see her while you are here. Inshalla." She waved them off so she could serve a growing line of hungry customers. Half of them called out greetings to Johanna and inquiries after the goods her father would be selling.

"Who's Fatima?" Jaufre said.

"Malala and Ahmed's daughter," Johanna said. "I've known her forever."

They stood next to the olive oil stall, tearing off chunks of warm naan to dip into the sample bowl and wolf it down. The olive oil man topped off the bowl and continued his pitch to the crowd. "The very finest olive oil to be had within a thousand leagues! The first pressing of the season, from the vineyards of Messenia! A delicate flavor and a sturdy body, perfect for both cooking and dressing!" He smiled benignly down at the two urchins with his product dripping off their chins. "And, ladies and gentlemen, the best prices this side of the Levant!" He leaned forward and said to Johanna, "Young miss, you will tell your father, the honorable Wu Li, that Yusuf the Levantine says this is the best press of oil in a generation, yes? The cooks of Cambaluc will pay any price for it."

Johanna nodded, her solemnity belied somewhat by the smearing of the best press of oil in a generation across her face with the back of her hand. "Be sure I will tell him so this evening, Yusuf."

He bowed, his hand on his heart. "Then I am content. Approach, good sirs, approach! Oil of Messenia, the first pressing! The taste, ah, the taste!" He kissed his fingers to the sky. "The taste will make you swoon!"

He winked at Johanna and she fainted dead away into the arms of a startled Jaufre, to the chuckles of the surrounding crowd.

After that they went to wool sheds to watch the sheep being shorn, where the shearer gave Johanna samples of this year's wool clip with an adjuration that she hand them over to Wu Li as soon as possible because everyone knew how fine was the wool harvested from the flocks of Ibrahim the Berber and his supply was already dangerously low. They proceeded to the cow barns to watch the auction, and then to the horse yard, where they spent the rest of the afternoon watching a group of men comprising three generations of the same family buy a small Arabian stallion with a hide as black as ebony, from another family of four generations. A representative of each generation from each family got to ride him the length of the yard and back again. He was a lovely sight, his graceful neck arched, his nose stretched out to drink the wind, his tail flying behind him as he seemed to float above the ground that passed so swiftly beneath his hooves. "See the tall man?" Johanna said. "The tallest man is always the broker."

"And if he isn't tall?" Jaufre said.

"Then he wears a tall hat," Johanna said.

They watched the tall man conduct the lengthy negotiations between the two parties, and as the sun slanted low over the white bulk of the Pamir Mountains a boy not much more than their own age was allowed to lead the stallion away, his face lit with joy and pride.

They returned to the caravansary at dusk, lips stained with pomegranate juice, oil on their chins and bread crumbs caught in the folds of their clothes. Jaufre, who had spent the day in a very good imitation of a carefree child, saw Wu Li and was recalled immediately to the fact of his recent history. The anxiety that made him seem so much older than his years settled over his features again.

Before he had to force himself to ask, Wu Li answered. "I'm sorry, Jaufre. There is still no word."

That evening, as the sun was just a memory in the western sky and the full moon only a pearly promise in the east, everyone staying in the caravansary gathered in the courtyard, around a large fire that had burned down to a circle of glowing coals. The members of the individual caravans grouped together to recline on blankets and lean against saddles. Everyone brought food and shared it, dumplings from Cambaluc, skewers of barbecued goat's liver from Yarkent, pickled eggs from Kuche, chicken tagines spiced with salty lemon from Maroc, black olives from Greece, the wonderful naan of Kashgar, all of it washed down with delicious sips of wine from Cyprus, decanted with pride from a wooden barrel by a trader who had brought it all the way from Antioch.

Jaufre, sitting miserable and silent behind Johanna, couldn't remember when the music began, or how, but at some point he became aware of words being sung, accompanied by an instrument of some kind. He looked up and saw four members of the caravan from Antioch, the one that had brought the wine from Cyprus, sitting together on a blanket placed near the fire so that its light could fall on their faces, eyes half closed. One voice was very deep, the other three much higher. They were accompanied by a fifth man on a wooden wind instrument with a flared lip, whose notes were sweet and plaintive.

It was a dialect of Persian with which he was unfamiliar, but after the first verse he began to catch the words. It was a marching song, sung by a caravaner always on the Road, the dust of the desert sticking in his throat, the thin air of the mountains leaving him gasping for breath, the pickpockets of Samarkand relieving him of what little money the girls of Trebizond had left behind. The Road was mother, went the chorus, the Road was father, the Road was sister, the Road was brother, the Road was home for such as they. The triumphant finish was greeted by enthusiastic applause, and one by one each of the companies stepped forward to sing their own songs, of first love, of lost love, of lost virginity, of ancient legends and not too modern wars, of the monsters that lurked in the dark around every corner of the Road. The Antioch caravan sang a forlorn song about a lost Jerusalem and the Tashkent caravan retaliated with a song about a pillaging group of ruthless Crusaders annihilated to the last man by righteous warriors of the Crescent. At the ending of each song both groups shouted good-natured insults that no one took seriously.

The moon was directly overhead by now and bright enough to cast long shadows in the courtyard. A group of Tuaregs assembled before the fire, their cheches wonderfully twisted and knotted about their heads, their hands and faces blue from the indigo dye that stained their clothes. They sat in a semicircle, each with his legs wrapped around skin drums of various sizes and graduated notes. One began a simple rhythm of single beats. After a moment or two a second drum joined in, countering the first's rhythm. A third rhythm wove joyfully above and below first and second. A fourth used his drum to back up a song in which he was instantly joined by his brethren. A fifth man shook heavy metal rattles in rhythm with the drums and began to dance around the circle and then into the seated audience, shaking his rattles and enticing them to join in. It wasn't hard, as even Jaufre couldn't keep his feet still.

Johanna noticed, and put her lips to his ear. "Do you know the song?"

He shook his head.

"They sing of Tin Hinan, the Tamenokalt from Tafilalt. A long time ago she united all the Tuaregs into one tribe. They call her 'the mother of us all.'" Her eyes sparkled in the firelight. "The song says that she is buried in a desert even larger than the Taklamakan, where the sand is red, not yellow, and the dunes are as high as mountains."

"You would like to see it," he said.

She looked surprised. "Of course. I want to see everything. Don't you?"

Before he could answer a cry went up. "Wu Li! Shu Ming! Young miss! Young miss! Young miss!"

Jaufre, surprised out of his misery, looked at his companions.

Wu Li rose to his feet and bowed, his face grave but his eyes twinkling. He raised Shu Ming to her feet with a courtly hand and led his family of three to the blanket by the fire. They settled down, Shu Ming plucking at the strings of a delicate lap harp, Wu Li with a small skin drum that produced a soft beat beneath the heels of his hands. Johanna sat before them, Shu Shao and Deshi the Scout arrayed themselves behind them, and the five voices blended as one. Wu Li's was low and mellow, Shu Ming's warm and feminine, Johanna's high and pure, Shu Shao and Deshi the Scout underpinning the rhythm in time with Wu Li's drum.

*White petals, soft scent*
*Friend of winter, summoner of spring*
*You leave us too soon.*

The camel drivers of Wu Li's caravan hummed the base note, giving it a rich, full presence in the still courtyard. The firelight flickered on the blue-tiled walls of the caravansary, looming up out of the dark all around them. The fountain tinkled, and the stars shone overhead in defiance of the radiant light of the moon.

Jaufre, listening, understood dimly that the song was not about a plum tree at all. Somehow, scarcely aware, the hard knot of agony and loss beneath his breastbone began to ease, just a little.

The next day Wu Li, having emptied the last pack of every item either brought with them from Cambaluc or acquired along the way, and having crossed and crossed again every street and alley of Kashgar where there was something for sale, began to entertain offers to buy or trade. Jaufre ushered the sellers into Wu Li's presence, and announced their names and their goods. He was alive to the importance of first impressions and took care with his bows and his manners.

Johanna stood at Wu Li's elbow, guardian of Wu Li's bao. This was a small jade cylinder with Chinese characters carved in bas relief on one end. When a deal was struck, Johanna would remove the lid from a tiny, shallow jade pot, revealing it to be filled with a red paste, which Jaufre later learned was a mixture of ground cinnabar, oil and threads of silk. Wu Li would press the end of the bao into the paste and stamp a small square of paper, upon which had been written the details of the deal just concluded with the merchant then before him.

The bao was Wu Li's seal, the three carved characters representing his family name and the words "trader" and "honest." The seal had been conferred on his father by the khan and was known from one end of the Road to the other and on all its various routes. It represented Wu Li's word and bond to deal fairly with all who did business with him. All sellers left Wu Li's tent clutching a square of paper with the agreed-upon figures scribbled on it and the stamp of the House of Wu in one corner, a guarantee of good faith payment immediately upon presentation. Most of them exchanged it for coin when Wu Li's men appeared to load the purchased goods onto a camel, but a seller could choose not to accept coin for his goods immediately. Instead, they might redeem the piece of paper a month or even a year from the day it was stamped, for coin or for goods of equal value, from Cipangu to Venice.

Yusuf the Levantine, self-confessed dealer in the very finest olive oil to be had within a thousand leagues, bewailed the price Wu Li refused to go above, but he winked at Jaufre on his way out, tucking his precious piece of paper securely into his sash.

Jaufre looked at Johanna. She smiled and stood even more proudly behind her father.

Three weeks after the caravan had arrived in Kashgar, they were making preparations to leave. Wu Li, Shu Ming, Shu Shao, and Deshi the Scout gathered in a group to debate the best, as in most profitable, route home.

Wu Li had acquired a new map from a local Kashgar dealer, an Arabic map drawn more than 170 years before according to the faded date in one corner. A name was barely legible in another. "Al-Idrisi," Johanna said haltingly, spelling it out out. Wu Li had been teaching her Arabic writing, and she looked at him to see how well she had done.

"Al-Idrisi," her father said. "All. E. Dree. Si."

"Al-Idrisi," Johanna said with more confidence.

The map was impressive in its clean lines and sharp geographical features and even more so in its startling lack of religious icons and exhortations. What Wu Li knew of it was accurate, something that could not often be said of any map not drawn by himself or his agents. It was a reproduction, of course, and the parchment crackled with age, but he and Johanna could easily adapt it into his route book.

The book was a collection of maps of all the routes Wu Li had ever traveled, some with his father and his father's great friend Marco Polo, but mostly they were from later travels of his own, bound in a small volume between supple calfskin stamped with his seal. One page led to another so that to follow—or retrace—a certain route all one had to do was turn the page forward or back. Each page was annotated in Wu Li's neat characters, the names of his agents in each location, the best vendors in oil and carpets and spices, the names of the more reasonable government officials along the way. Or the more reasonably priced ones.

The route book was every bit as valuable a possession as Wu Li's bao, compiled over twenty years of almost constant travel. They consulted it now in a body, himself, Shu Ming, Shu Shao, Deshi the Scout, and Johanna, with Jaufre sitting behind her, a fascinated if slightly unwilling auditor. After all, he thought, it wasn't as if he was going with them.

"We should take the southern route home," Shu Shao said.

"You never want to miss the spice market, Shasha," Johanna said.

Shasha smiled but did not deny it.

"It is true," Deshi the Scout said. "Spices are small and light and very valuable for their weight."

Deshi the Scout was always in favor of any commodity that was easy to pack and that would not weigh down the camels on the Road, especially not on the Road home.

"Nutmeg," Shu Ming murmured. It was the most precious of spices in the East, revered by any cook worthy of the name, and was held by healers to have medicinal properties as well.

"There is all the nutmeg one could want in Kinsai," Wu Li said.

Shu Shao smiled. "We are not in Kinsai," she said.

Wu Li looked around the circle and laughed. "Is it a conspiracy, then?" Without waiting for an answer he gave a decisive nod. "The southern route, then, through Yarkent." He shook his head. "Other than the oil, we have picked up very little in bulk here in Kashgar." He looked at Deshi the Scout. "We should make good time."

Deshi the Scout nodded.

"I have some news good enough to make us all sleep easier on the Road," Wu Li said. "Ogodei and his ten thousand accompany us at least as far as Yarkent."

Wu Li saw Shu Ming's shoulders relax. The memories of Jaufre's caravan must have been preying on her mind. Well, and they had preyed upon his own.

She looked up and saw him watching her, and knew her thoughts to be his own. She smiled at him.

"And after Yarkent?" Wu Li said. "Straight home to Cambaluc?"

There seemed to be no objection. Wu Li dismissed them to their various chores, and he and Johanna settled in to transferring the information from the new map into Wu Li's route book. There were no roads on it, of course, and much of the distance involved had to be guessed at, but Johanna yearned for what lay at the edges of the pages. Wu Li gave an indulgent laugh. "We will travel them all one day," he told her.

"To the ends of the pages?" she said, her eyes drawn to the islands floating off the western edge of the map.

He tousled her hair. "To the ends of the earth itself," he said.

She beamed up at him, and Jaufre knew a moment's envy, not only for Johanna's possession of a father still living, but for the prospect of a shore not yet seen.

Wu Li was supervising the padding and packing of the two dozen amphorae of oil the next day when he felt a plucking at his elbow. He turned and saw a city clerk, an older man bent and shortsighted from years of stooping over his accounts. "Tabari," he said, inclining his head courteously. "Forgive me, I did not see you standing there. How may I help you?"

He listened to Tabari's hurried speech with a bent head. Shu Ming, on the other side of the courtyard, saw the gathering frown beneath his polite expression.

Tabari brought news of a beautiful woman who had fetched the highest price that year on the Kashgar slave block. He knew the names of several people who had attended the auction, and after suitable reward shared them with Wu Li.

After an afternoon and a following morning spent knocking on Kashgar doors, bribes in hand, the one man Wu Li could find who would admit to having been present and who was willing to describe what had happened rolled his eyes and patted his heart. "Ah, you should have seen her, my friend! Not young, no, but ripe enough that the juice would run down your chin when you took a bite. Eyes so dark and liquid you could imagine diving into them, hair like black silk, and a figure—" his hands sketched an improbable shape in the air "—Oh, my friend. A proud one, too, head high, unashamed, though they stripped her for the bidding. It was fierce, I will tell you." He sighed reminiscently.

If only Barid the Balasagan's purse had measured up to his appreciation for a beautiful woman, it was clear that Wu Li's search would have ended there. Barid winked at Wu Li and gave him a nudge with his elbow. "But I know you for a stolid married man these many years, my friend. What is this, that you ask after another woman? If she knew, Shu Ming would carve out your liver and eat it while you bled to death in front of her, eh? What? A name?" He scratched his head. "Was she the one they called the Rose of Jordan? No, no, that was that skinny girl with the missing teeth. I think they called this one the Lycian Lotus. Eh? Who won? Some sheik from the west, I heard. Bedu, Turgesh." He gave a vague wave of his hand, indicating everything west of Kashgar. "Berber, maybe. No, I didn't catch his name. What? Who sold her?" He scratched his chin. "Anwar the Egyptian. At least he was the one looking the most satisfied at the end of the day. It's wonderful how he manages to offer the primest of prime goods every time, eh?"

Not so wonderful, if Anwar the Egyptian worked as a receiver of stolen goods for Persian raiders, Wu Li thought.

Anwar the Egyptian was brusque. "She was only one of a group I bought two days before. Her buyer?" He eyed Wu Li. "Honorable Wu Li, of course I wish to be of help, but—thank you." A jingle of coin. "Yes, I remember now. A sheik from the west. I don't remember his name."

Wu Li doubted that. "Where in the west?" he said.

The slaver shrugged. "It is a vast area, the west. Many places, many people." His smile did not reach his eyes. "Many sheiks."

Wu Li suppressed a sigh and reached again into his purse.

Anwar the Egyptian eyed the coin, gold this time, that Wu Li was fingering. "He said something about one more stop on his way home, to pick up a new sword."

"Do you think it was her?" Shu Ming said that evening.

"She matches Jaufre's description, but then so does every other woman between here and Antioch."

"Lycia is a place in Greece," Shu Ming said. "I think. Or near it."

"Yes," Wu Li said. "And he says his mother was Greek."

"And a new sword for someone rich enough to pay that much for a slave means Damascus," Shu Ming said. "How far away is Damascus?"

"Two thousand leagues and more," Wu Li said. "Too far."

They sat in heavy silence for a moment.

"You'll have to tell him."

"Yes." But he didn't stir.

"What troubles you, my husband?"

"You remember why I wanted her to have a western name?"

She was startled by what seemed to be an abrupt change of subject, because Wu Li always spoke to the purpose. "Johanna?"

He nodded. "Johanna," he said. He smiled a little. "Wu Johanna."

She smiled, too, at the incongruity, at the odd conjoining of east and west in a single name. "Of course I remember," she said. "She looks western." As I do, she could have said. "Her grandfather is seen in her face for any who look upon her." She laid a hand on his arm. "I agreed with you, Li. Her face already sets her apart. It would have been silly, even cruel, to put a Chinese name to that face."

He nodded, his hand coming up to clasp hers. "But it is more than that, Ming. You have seen as well as I the change. In spite of the Khan's efforts, fear and hatred of foreigners grows in Cambaluc, more every year. I have even heard talk of expelling them all, of closing the ports to foreign ships."

She knew what he said was true, and said nothing.

"I fear Johanna will never find a home in Cambaluc," he said. "I feared it when she was born. I wanted her to have a name she could wear easily if..."

"If she lived somewhere other than Cambaluc."

He let out a long, slow sigh. "Yes."

She was silent for a moment. "She wants him to stay with us."

"I know," Wu Li said. "I like what I see of the boy."

"As do I."

"And I was thinking that it would be good for her to have someone, a companion who looks like her—"

A brother, Shu Ming thought. The brother I could not give her. The son I could not give you.

"—a friend who will walk with her through the years. She will have all I own, but I fear it will not be enough. She is too foreign. She could be married for my fortune, and disposed of when we are gone."

They sat in silence for a few moments, and then Wu Li rose to his feet. "But you are right, my wife. I must tell him. The decision must be his."

Jaufre listened in solemn silence, Johanna sitting close by his side. In the past weeks, the two had grown inseparable. "I am sorry, Jaufre," Wu Li said. "There is no more to be done."

The boy's face was white and strained. Johanna, looking at him anxiously, understood. Both of his parents had been alive and whole and present a month before. She looked at her mother and her father sitting across from them, the tea tray between them forgotten by them all.

Into the silence, Wu Li said, "I understand your need to find her, Jaufre, and it does you credit. But she could be anywhere now, and there is no place even for you to begin to look. 'A sheik in the west' is not helpful. There are hundreds of sheiks. Thousands. And your own father owned a blade of Damascus steel."

Wu Li glanced at Johanna, whose eyes were raised trustfully to his face. Just so had Jaufre no doubt once looked at his father, with absolute faith, certain that he could make all well. "This is my thought," he said. "My daughter and my wife, I myself have come to value you highly. Shu Shao and Deshi the Scout both speak well of you, and I value their counsel. There is a place for you in our family. Return with us to Cambaluc, and let yourself grow into a man." Wu Li sighed. "And when that day comes, set out in search of your mother, if it is what you still wish to do."

The cry was wrenched from him. "She could be dead by then, Wu Li!"

"She could be dead now." Wu Li felt Shu Ming's eyes upon him. This was unlikely, they both knew. Anyone who had paid the price quoted by an awed Barid the Balasagan would have taken very great care of so valuable a property, but if Jaufre set out in pursuit he would be dead shortly thereafter of any one of a number of causes, or a slave himself, in which case his mother would be dead to him and he to her for all time. The world was vast and travel across it slow. Chances were weighted heavily against mother and son ever meeting again, but any small hope Jaufre had of it lay in joining the Wu household.

And this, Jaufre, displaying what would become a lifelong ability to recognize the truth, however unpalatable it was and however much it cost him, came to understand for himself. When they left Kashgar three days later, he rode behind Johanna, swaying over the sand on the back of the young camel.

If he looked over his shoulder too often, surely no one was so cruel as to mention it.

# · Five ·

1320 A.D.
*Cambaluc*

⊢——⊣

The route to Cipangu to trade silk for pearls, initiated by Wu Hai and carried forward with efficiency and dispatch by Wu Li, had become an annual event in the trading house of Wu. This had been a most profitable year, partially due, Wu Li had to admit, if only to himself, to Johanna's ability to make friends wherever she went. In this case she had ingratiated herself into the society of the women pearl divers of Ama, who had taught her the art of holding her breath underwater for a long enough time as to strike terror into the hearts of her parents waiting anxiously on shore. But what could they do?

"She's too old to scold and too tall to beat," Wu Li said ruefully.

His wife gave him a fond look. "As if you have ever done either."

By the time they reached the Edo docks, Wu Li was concerned enough over the value of their cargo that he hired another half dozen guards from the always steady supply found on any port. One, a youngish thickset man whose black quilted armor and well-kept naginata argued a fall from samurai grace, was so anxious to board ship that he accepted the first salary offer Wu Li made. By the time they reached Kinsai, having proved his value in two encounters with pirates, he was outspoken in his belief that he was deserving of a bonus amounting to twenty-five percent of the value of the trade goods he had helped to protect. He said so, loudly, and this sounded like a fine idea to the other Nippon guards Wu Li had hired in Edo. They stood in front of him in a half-circle, hands resting on their weapons in a manner completely lacking in subtlety.

"The value of your contribution to the success of our voyage is not in dispute, Gokudo," Wu Li said, answering threat with courtesy. "Indeed, it was my intention to pay you a bonus of ten percent of the worth of the goods you have helped us shepherd safely to port. However."

His eyes hardened and he made a motion with one hand. Deshi the Scout and a dozen other retainers materialized behind the Nippon guards, armed with swords, pry bars and belaying pins.

"Because of your greed," Wu Li said, courtesy giving way to contempt, "and your inability to make your case for reimbursement without threat, you will receive the salary we agreed on in Edo, and not one tael more."

There was the promise of an incipient riot, but Wu Li's men were in sufficient number to quell it before the Mongol authorities were alerted and all his profit went in fines for failure to keep the peace. "My thanks, Deshi," Wu Li said, and for the first time noticed that the scout was pale and shivering. "My friend, you are ill! Return home at once and seek out Shu Shao. She will know what to do."

Unfortunately, in this instance, Shu Shao, already a healer of some repute, did not.

The next morning, Shu Ming fell ill. She complained of loose stool in the morning, and three hours later she, too, was pale and shivering, her skin clammy to the touch, her heart hammering beneath her skin at a frantic, irregular pace. She complained of thirst, when her mind wasn't wandering, which it did more and more as the day wore on. They tried giving her clear soup and tea but she couldn't keep anything down, and by the afternoon her sodden bedclothes had to be changed every hour.

Before nightfall, she was dead.

So was the maid who laundered her sheets, the stable boy, Deshi the Scout, and 3,526 other citizens of Cambaluc.

In the horrible weeks that followed, Wu Li went about looking like a ghost. Johanna attended him white-lipped and withdrawn. Jaufre suffered the loss of his second mother with outward calm and inward agony, taking over the mews and the stables while Shu Shao took charge of the kitchen, and all went on tiptoe for fear that the master of the house would shatter like glass at one wrong word.

One day a month later Jaufre went out to the stables and found Johanna seated on a bale of hay next to Edyk the Portuguese, deep in earnest conversation. She looked more animated than she had since the day her mother died. Edyk was holding one of Johanna's hands in both of his own, and as Jaufre came around the corner he raised it to his lips.

Johanna looked up and saw Jaufre. She pulled her hand free and jumped to her feet. "Edyk has come."

"So I see." The two men exchanged a cool glance.

"I am sorry for the trouble that has visited the house of the Honorable Wu Li," Edyk said with a formal bow.

Jaufre inclined his head a fraction. He could not rue the lightening of sorrow on Johanna's face, even if he suspected that their recent troubles were not what had brought Edyk the Portuguese to the house of Wu Li.

Edyk the Portuguese was in his early twenties and, like Johanna and Jaufre, the child of expatriate Westerners, with eyes too round for Cambaluc comfort. A brawny young man, thickly-muscled, again like Johanna and Jaufre he moved with the assurance of someone accustomed to an active life. He had his father's brown eyes and his mother's black hair and a charming smile all his own. He was a trader, as the honorable Wu Li had been a trader, and traveling the trade routes with him Johanna had watched that smile melt feminine hearts from Kinsai to Kashgar.

He was shorter than Jaufre by a head, which was some comfort to the crusader's son, but he made up for his lack of height with a dynamic personality and a great deal of personal charm and energy. He was an up-and-coming merchant in Cambaluc, one of the group of foreign traders resident there by permission of the Khan who accounted for the bulk of foreign goods imported into the city. Since the death of the Great Khan, raiders on the Silk Road had moved from a rarity to a steadily increasing threat. In response, the Cambaluc merchants had banded together in a cooperative association, exchanging information on road conditions and organizing communal caravans at set times during the year. Pooling their resources, they could hire more guards, which increased their chances of a safe arrival at their destination, alive and with their goods intact, and, when they had finished their trading, a safe return home. Their profit would be less from the increased competition at their destinations, but at least they were sure of living to travel and trade another day.

The Honorable Wu Li had been among the proponents of this cooperative, and Edyk the Portuguese had been among the first to join. Young, only five years older than Jaufre and Johanna, intelligent, talented and ambitious, he was quick to see the benefits of Wu Li's proposal, and a caravan traveling under Wu Li's direction hadn't left Cathay in the last three years in which Edyk the Portuguese had not been a full partner, carrying silk west and driving a carefully selected group of purebred horses east. He favored Arabians, but when available he did not turn up his nose at draft horses like the Ardennais, mules, and the occasional zebra, which could be bred with horses to make a hardy pony good for narrow trails at high elevations, a breed championed by a certain faction of Mongol nobles who were willing to pay any amount to acquire better transportation for their troops.

He'd met Johanna during the Cambaluc merchants' first communal caravan, early one morning when he'd come down to inspect his father's picket line and had found her galloping up on his most obstreperous stallion. "His front right shoe is a little loose, I think," she had said without introduction, and slid from the stallion's back to pick up his right front foot, beckoning Edyk closer for an inspection of the offending shoe. She had been right.

Edyk's father had been a rogue Cistercian monk, born in Portugal, who had abandoned a life of contemplation and cloister for one of travel and adventure. Like Johanna's grandfather, upon reaching the East he had offered his services to the court of the Great Khan. Those services had been able enough to achieve recognition and reward, again like Johanna's grandfather, in the form of Edyk the Portuguese's mother, the daughter of a Chinese concubine. Again, like Johanna and Jaufre, by virtue of his foreign blood he was shunned by Cambaluc society, and not much more welcomed by the ruling class.

Foreign traders, the proximate cause of so much Mongol wealth, were regarded as somewhere in between, and their children, especially the children of favorite foreigners and ex-Mongol concubines, were even then regarded as a breed apart, not quite other but not quite equal, either. Like Johanna and Jaufre and lacking an alternative, Edyk was drawn to others of his kind.

Where Johanna went Jaufre followed and the three of them had become nearly inseparable over the years, but recently Jaufre had noticed a change in Edyk's manner toward Johanna, less brotherly and more, well, affectionate, was the only word for it. It set Jaufre's teeth on edge.

"North Star's foal was born last night," Edyk said.

In spite of himself, Jaufre brightened. "All well?"

Edyk grinned. "He was running before he could walk. A winner, I'll wager."

And he would, Jaufre thought, and Edyk the Portuguese would win, too. Upon succeeding to his father's business three years before, Edyk had shifted emphasis from general goods to livestock, in particular racing stock, and had made a name for himself in buying and backing winners.

"And North Star?" Johanna said.

"Well, though I think this is the last time I will breed her. She has done enough for my stables."

"What are you calling him?"

Edyk smiled at her. She was taller than he was but it didn't seem to bother him. "What would you like me to call her, Golden Flower?"

Jaufre didn't like the caressing tone in his voice, and still less did he like Edyk's employment of Johanna's Cambaluc name. "What color is his coat?"

Edyk's smile lessened. "He is pure white, nose to tail."

A short silence fell. They all knew that white was the color of death. Johanna and Jaufre were still wearing white in honor of Shu Ming's death, although they would be putting it off when the month of official mourning had passed. "Will Chinese gamblers bet on a white horse?" Jaufre said.

"They will on this one," Edyk said with more assurance. "And Mongol gamblers certainly will. We're just lucky it's a colt and not a filly."

Johanna and even Jaufre in spite of himself nodded emphatic agreement. A vast herd of white mares was maintained by the Mongol emperor for the production and fermenting of their milk. If North Star had born a female, Edyk would have been expected to gift it to the Mongol court, no matter how fast a foal out of North Star might be expected to run. Koumiss was more of a staple in the Mongolian diet than bread or meat.

"Then call him North Wind," Johanna said. "Let him be named for how fast he will run."

A slow smile spread across Edyk's face. "Perfect," he said, and swung Johanna up into his arms and whirled her around.

Jaufre, watching, schooled his expression to something that felt a little less like murder.

On the other side of Cambaluc, where families who could trace their ancestries back to the Shang dynasty lived closely together in a section renowned for its insularity, xenophobia and self-regard, another meeting was taking place, with consequences reaching much farther than the selection of a lucky name for a winning horse.

The house was every bit as large as its neighbors, but its appearance had declined with the fortunes of its owners. Luck had not followed the Dai family for three generations. Once one of the richest trading concerns in Everything Under the Heavens, the hopes of everyone under the Dai roof were now vested in the person of Dai Fang, an exquisite beauty of twenty years. Like Johanna, she was the only child of her house. Her mother was an invalid, her father inconstant, and when one day at the age of fifteen Dai Fang discovered that the only food in the house was two eggs laid by a stringy hen who had then immediately died, she had shut her father in a room with the cheapest bottle of rice wine she could find and had stepped forward to take the reins of the family business into her own hands.

Over the past five years, those hands had proved to be capable. Intelligent and ruthless, with an invaluable talent for identifying well in advance of demand that one luxury item that the wives and concubines of Cambaluc simply could not do without that year. Allied with a charm of manner that had seduced many an older trader with more experience and a much harder head, Dai Fang made agreements and partnerships profitable enough to draw the Dai fortunes back up over the edge of disaster. When she had balanced the books at the end of the previous year, for the first time in four years the knot in her belly eased a little. They would not starve. The house would not have to be sold to pay their debts. Her mother could have the services of a decent nurse, who could also provide herbal remedies for Dai Yu's own needs. If disaster in the form of sandstorm or flood or raiders did not descend upon next year's caravan, the house of Dai might even see a profit. A modest one, to be sure, but encouraging after so many years of loss.

It was at this inopportune moment that her father sobered up enough to notice that his daughter had reached the venerable age of twenty without being married. Unable to bear the shame, he entered into an arrangement with a matchmaker and began interviewing prospective sons-in-law. This was not to Dai Fang's taste at all, not least because of Gokudo, her father's Nippon sergeant of the guard, hired for a pittance a year before.

"He will never allow you to marry me," Gokudo said. Twenty-six, a hard-muscled man of middle height, his hands were rough and calloused from work with the spear with the curved blade he called the naginata, the weapon he only put down when he joined Dai Fang in her bed. Even now, it leaned against the wall within easy reach.

"No," she said. "The honorable Dai Fu would be horrified at the very thought of joining the revered house of Dai with a man not born in Everything Under the Heavens."

He looked down at her, his amusement showing in his face.

"What?"

He shook his head. Far be it from him to draw her attention to the fact that the honorable Dai Fu's daughter shared her bed, enthusiastically and without inhibition, with a man not himself born in Everything Under the Heavens. A warrior nobleman exiled from his own country, he was still a foreigner here, forced to sell his services as a lowly bodyguard to a failed merchant, a man whom he would never even have met, let alone associated with were he still heir to those rights, privileges and duties conferred by five hundred generations of birth, influence and favor.

But then taking a lover was of much less importance than taking a husband.

He took a deep, steadying breath, calming yet again the shame and the fury that burned always in his breast. His father had picked the losing side in a struggle for power and their family was no more. It was futile to dwell on the past, although the day would come when…Again he forced away thoughts of vengeance and retribution. They were a waste of energy best spent elsewhere.

And there were compensations to his present occupation, to be sure. Slowly he drew back the coverlet and let himself enjoy the sight of her smooth, unblemished skin, the small, ruby-crowned breasts, the mystery between her lissome legs concealed by a tight weave of black hair. He had trimmed that cap of hair himself, with a sharp knife and infinite care. As he watched, she stretched, opening her legs, legs that ended in tiny, folded-back feet that had been bound since birth, a grotesquerie that had charmed him at first sight.

A delicate film of moisture made her skin glow in the moonlight. He felt his body respond, and he smiled. After all, what need had Dai Fang of sure feet? It was off them that he liked her best. And if she married judiciously...

He looked up to meet her eyes as his hand traveled up the inside of her thigh. "Then we must select the proper husband for you."

She sighed, arching her back. "And you have some suggestions along those lines, I suspect."

He was on her and in her, ferocious, sudden, his hand clapping brutally over her mouth as she cried out in surprise. "As it happens."

Servicing his mistress required only the attention of his body, and left his mind free to plot the various ways he could bring Dai Fang's attention to the newly bereaved state of that most prosperous Cambaluc merchant, the honorable Wu Li.

In the end the choice was obvious, and Dai Fu required very little persuading to open negotiations. The honorable Wu Li was of impeccable lineage with extensive holdings who had recently lost his wife and who had no son. There was of course the matter of having looked outside his race for his first wife, but that could be excused on the grounds of his father's misplaced loyalty to an absent associate, an honorable if foolish act. Dai Fang was a young woman of excellent family and considerable beauty. It took very little encouragement for Dai Fang to arrange a meeting between her father and the honorable Wu Li, a meeting at which she contrived to be present. He wasn't interested until she allowed herself to display some knowledge of trade. Further questions, delicately put beneath Dai Fu's benevolent if slightly drunken eye, revealed a shrewd mind, wrapped in a traditional and delightfully feminine package.

In appearance she was as unlike Shu Ming as she could be, and so Wu Li overlooked her bound feet, and the calculating look in her eyes.

The matter was arranged in a week. The sensation this caused in Wu Li's household lasted longer than that, but by not so much as the lift on an eyebrow did Dai Fang reveal any knowledge of the information the spies in the honorable Wu Li's house reported daily to Gokudo. Her plans were laid and Wu Li so completely in her thrall that she felt confident that she would be able to see them through.

The marriage took place a month later. Dai Fang's mother's nurse, an invaluable consultant, was able to supply her with an effective means of convincing Wu Li of her innocence. He was entirely beguiled, displaying a tenderness for her that first night that was as touching as it was tedious.

She left the nurse with her mother, but she took Gokudo with her as her personal bodyguard when she moved into Wu Li's house.

And so infatuated with his new wife was Wu Li that he did not recognize Gokudo as the guard he had hired in Edo at the end of his last voyage to Cipangu.

# · Six ·

1322 A.D.
*Cambaluc*

⊢——⊣

"My husband is dead," the widow said.

Not "Your father." Not the more formal "The head of the house of Wu." Just the exclusive, proprietary "My husband." The widow was selfish even in her alleged grief.

There was also a hard glitter of triumph in her dark eyes, for those with the wit to see it.

"I know," the girl said. The words were calm, devoid of grief or sorrow, devoid, indeed, of any expression at all.

The widow's mouth tightened into a lacquered red line. "How?" She had forbidden any communication between the mongrel's servants and her own, on pain of severe punishment.

The girl shrugged without answering. Her eyes met the widow's without expression, without humility and, most inexcusably, without fear.

The widow felt the familiar rage well up in her breast. Her hands trembled with it, curling into claws, the resemblance enhanced by the long, enameled fingernails. She saw the little mongrel looking at them, still with no expression on her alien face, and inhaled slowly, straightening her fingers from claws into hands once more.

Behind her Gokudo stirred, a brief movement, a rustle of clothing, but it was enough to remind her of what was at stake. The little mongrel still had friends at court, associates of Wu Li who remembered him with respect and fondness and who might be persuaded to listen to any grievances Wu Li's daughter might have with her father's second wife.

Gokudo was of course quite correct. The Khan's attention must be avoided, and it required only her own self-control. The widow caused her rage to abate by sheer willpower, until she was able to look on her husband's daughter and only child with at least the appearance of indifference. Soon the little mongrel would be out of the house and out of her life.

The mongrel wasn't little, being indecently tall, towering over everyone in the house and over most of the citizens of Cambaluc for that matter, but the widow never thought of her any other way. The little mongrel was nothing but a blight on the honored ancestors of the house of Wu, upon the sacred ancestors of Everything Under the Heavens itself, and what was worse, the little mongrel cost more than any two other members of the household to feed and clothe. Since the widow had cajoled her honorable husband Wu Li into letting her take over his accounts after his accident, she knew just how much extra silk it took to keep the length of the little mongrel's legs and arms decently covered, and how many bowls of noodles it took to fill her apparently bottomless belly.

If the little mongrel's size had not damned her beyond redemption, her features surely would have. Her eyes were not a decent, modest brown or culturally acceptable black but instead a blue so light the irises were almost gray, with no hint of fold in the eyelid. The little mongrel lacked even the common courtesy to drop her gaze out of respect in the presence of her elders, and especially her betters.

And as tightly confined as fashion and tradition decreed in a single braid that reached her waist, the little mongrel's hair was still as unruly and unmanageable as the little mongrel herself, escaping a wisp at a time to curl round the pale face with its odd cheekbones, enormous nose and grossly oversized mouth. The hair had not even the saving grace of color, that thick rich black fall of hair one might expect of the honorable Wu Li's daughter, but instead a brown streaked with bronze, acquired during the improperly hatless and shockingly astride daily rides with her father and that foreign stableboy the honorable Wu Li had so carelessly chosen first as his daughter's playmate and later as her personal guard. Perhaps Wu Li had felt that the essential outlandishness in each made them fit only for their own company. Certainly they were inseparable.

Wu Li's widow was pleased enough with this reasoning to ignore the presence of Gokudo at her shoulder. He was the noble warrior of an honorable race strong enough to defeat two invasions by Kublai Khan himself, not to be compared to the descendant of a race of men who could not hold a land they had conquered for even fifty years.

The little mongrel's stepmother averted her eyes before her inventory could take in the abomination of close-cut fingernails and unbound feet, but she was shocked to her very soul at such an unfeminine disregard for the proprieties. That the little mongrel herself was without sense or shame was expected but that Wu Li would have allowed either was unbelievable. Foreign, the widow thought with an inward shudder, the most insulting epithet in her language.

Yes, in birth, appearance and demeanor, altogether an unsatisfactory little mongrel to dispose of, but disposed of she must be if the widow wished to gather the reins of her husband's importing business into her own supremely competent hands, and that she most certainly wished to do.

All that remained was the safe disposition of the sole heir of Wu Li's body.

Fortunately a solution to the problem was ready to hand. The widow smiled to herself, and said, "Ceremonies for your father will take place three days from now." She paused, and added with a bow that was as patronizing as it was slight, "You may attend."

The little mongrel displayed no proper gratitude for the magnanimity thus offered. There was no bow of acknowledgement, no polite murmur of appreciation. Her blue-gray eyes remained steady on the widow's face. Truth be told, that unflinching gaze was a little unnerving.

Again, Gokudo shifted behind the widow. Her eyes moved to the marble-topped table reposing in isolated splendor against one wall. On its carved and polished top rested two items, carefully centered. One was the jade box that held Wu Li's bao. The other was the fat leather-bound journal that held the names of all of Wu Li's agents in cities far and near, and his annotated maps of trading routes as far as the Middle Sea. The power these two items represented was enough to soothe her irritation.

She turned her head to see the little mongrel watching her. She dropped her eyes and smoothed the heavy blue silk of her dress. "There is another matter we must discuss. Sit down." She beckoned a servant forward with one graceful sweep of a hand heavy with rings. "Will you have tea?"

The girl folded her long frame down onto a pillow, crossing her legs and resting a hand on each knee, instead of kneeling with bent head and clasped hands in an attitude of proper attentiveness. She refused tea. Impolite and graceless as well as ugly, the widow noted, not without pleasure.

They waited as the tea was poured and the servant retired. The widow sipped delicately at the fragrant liquid in the paper-thin porcelain cup. After a moment of appreciative contemplation of the delicate design traced on its rim, she said, her tone casual, "I have received an offer of marriage for you."

"Have you?" The strange light eyes met hers. "From whom?"

The widow allowed herself a small, playful smile. "It is from the son of Maffeo the Portuguese."

The blue eyes widened so slightly that if the widow had not been watching so closely for any change of expression she would have missed it. "Is it?" was all the little mongrel said.

"It is, and a very generous offer, too," her father's widow said. "He offers silk, spices, an interest in future trading ventures."

"Generous indeed," the little mongrel said, after a moment.

"And of course you have known each other since you were children."

"Of course."

Her stepmother looked up suspiciously but could perceive no sarcasm in that clear, alien gaze. She folded her tiny hands in her lap and regarded their long polished nails, longer than the fingers themselves, with thoughtful attention. "Altogether a most suitable match."

"Isn't it, though," the little mongrel said, her tone almost amiable.

Her father's widow smiled again, broadly this time. "Then, if you have no objection, I will put the matter in hand at once."

"As you wish, my father's second wife," the girl said.

Again her stepmother looked sharply for guile in those strange eyes. She found none. It was not that she had expected outright opposition, but she had been spiteful enough to hope that some aspect of the little mongrel's planned future would be displeasing to her. Instead, the girl seemed acquiescent, amenable even, to be disposed of so quickly and so efficiently.

It was with a faint feeling of disappointment that she terminated the interview, and turned with relief to the affairs of her husband's trading empire.

Hers now.

# · Seven ·

⊢——⊣

**P**ride kept Johanna's departing step to a stroll much slower than her usual ground-eating stride. The widow's creature scowled and closed the door so swiftly and so firmly behind her that her robe nearly caught in the crack. She paused for a moment to consider it, the heavy mahogany panels carved with the symbols for health and prosperity, the massive bronze ring pulls.

The heavy bronze lock.

The door had been closed against her, to keep her out, to separate her from her father and, more importantly, any claim on his estate. She understood that quite well.

She smiled. It would never occur to the widow or her Nipponese creature that the barrier of the door worked both ways.

She turned and made straight for her own suite, the two small rooms in the back of the house to which she had been relegated upon the occasion of her father's remarriage. If asked, Johanna would have replied truthfully that she preferred her new location, as it was closer to the stables, the mews and the kitchen, and horses, falcons and food ranked very high in importance in her life. Her lyra she kept next to her bed, so that music was never out of her reach.

Once in her room she threw off the heavy silk robe, the wonderfully embroidered Robe of a Thousand Larks that had once belonged to her mother, that she had donned for the visit of state to her father's second wife, and pulled on trousers and tunic made of heavier raw silk. It was dyed a rich black and trimmed with dull black sateen. Black for travel, not white for mourning. She had been adamant in the face of Shasha's remonstrations. She would not at this late date bow to the traditions of a place that had treated her like an outsider all her life.

She smoothed one hand over the nubbled texture. She had bargained for the fabric herself, on their last trip to Suchow. The blue-gray eyes went blank for a moment and she stood still, unmoving, staring at nothing.

She shook herself out of her reverie and raised her voice. "Shasha? Where are you?"

"In the kitchen."

Shu Shao, now a kitchen drudge, was stirring a steaming pot over the stove. She looked up, ran her eyes over the girl's tall form, and said, "I remember the trip to Shandong with your father to buy that silk. It was the first time he permitted you to conduct the bargaining."

"I remember," Johanna said. Unable yet to bring herself to speak casually of her father, she gestured at the empty kitchen. "Where is everyone?"

Shasha snorted. "Over in her quarters."

"You can't blame them, Shasha," Johanna said. "They have to eat." She smiled. "And it will be easier for us to talk."

Shasha's brown eyes were as keen and clever as ever between their narrow lids. She examined the girl before her. "So?"

"So, we go."

Shasha felt a loosening of the apprehension that had been slowly accumulating since Wu Li had brought home his second wife. "When?"

"Three days. After the cremation."

"So soon?"

"It must be." Johanna grimaced. "She has arranged a marriage for me."

"Who?"

"Edyk."

Shasha's lids drooped until she looked half asleep. She resumed her stirring. "Hmmm."

"What is that supposed to mean?"

"What?"

"That 'hmmm'. You 'hmmm' and you nod to yourself. I hate it when you do that."

Shasha lifted the spoon out of the pot and setting it to one side. "He does love you."

"I know that," Johanna said. "I love him. It doesn't matter. It wouldn't work."

"You think not?"

There was as much pain as there was certainty in Johanna's reply. "I know not."

Shasha nodded again. She moved the pot to the back of the stove and reached for two bowls. "Bird's nest."

"My favorite."

The woman and the girl ate in companionable silence. Johanna asked for more and Shasha took great pleasure in filling the bowl to its rim for the second time.

"What?" Johanna said, catching sight of her expression.

Shasha shook her head. Wu Li's widow's complaints that Johanna ate twice as much as the hungriest horse in the stables lent spice to every bite of food the girl took. Shasha was willing to admit it lent a certain zest to ladling it out, too.

Johanna finished her third helping, set her bowl aside and stretched. She met the older woman's eyes with a gravity that sat heavily on her young features. "I must show you something, Shasha," she said.

She led the way to her bedroom, going straight to the silken tapestry hanging above her bed, caught up one corner and without hesitation ripped out the lining. Six small packages fell to the bed, each was wrapped in translucent rice paper and tied with string. With a certain solemn ceremoniousness in her manner she untied the string and unfolded the paper. She tilted the package and a gleaming stream of stones fell out, so deeply red they seemed as if they might set the coverlet on fire. Indeed, Shasha picked up one of the stones and where the gem rested her skin felt near to scorching. "From Mien," she said, and it wasn't a question. She let the stone slip from her hand back to the patched and faded coverlet.

"Yes," the girl said. She stirred the little heap of gems with a pensive forefinger. "We were coming home on the Grand Canal from Kinsai. The night before we started, this funny little man in a dhow tied up next to us." She smiled at the memory. "All those junks, and his was the only dhow. We had never seen one so far from Calicut before. Father invited him on board for dinner and when he realized I was a girl he dropped his jib and tied it round him with one of the jib sheets." At Shasha's puzzled look she smiled. "All he wore for traveling was a turban, you see."

Shasha laughed.

"His name was Lundi. He had a hooded snake he kept in a basket that lapped milk out of a saucer like a cat. He drank too much wine after dinner and started telling the story about Princess Padmini of Rajputana and the Moslem invader Ala-ud-din, only the way he told it Ala-ud-din got to Rajputana before Padmini killed herself. I could tell Father was about to send me to bed when Lundi's turban fell off and all these rubies fell out. It was like the story of From-Below-the-Steps and the night it rained emeralds. They were so beautiful. Father bought all of them on the spot."

Johanna smiled again. "Edyk said the last time he was in Kinsai that Lundi had bought a house by the river and filled the garden with hooded snakes and the house with pretty concubines, all named Padmini."

They stood in silence, staring down as the fiery swath of color glittering up at them. Johanna put her arm around the older woman's shoulders. "Some in the hems of my clothes, some in yours, some in Jaufre's. We leave in three days."

"Does she—"

"She knows nothing of them. Father gave them to me and told me to hide them." Her expression was bleak. "He said he thought I might need them one day."

"Well," Shasha said, voice very dry, "at least the man wasn't a complete fool."

There was a brief, taut silence. "Never speak of my father in that way again, Shasha," Johanna said. "Do you understand me?"

Oh, I understand perfectly, Shu Shao thought. "He was only a man, Johanna, and he was so lonely and so lost after Shu Ming died. And Dai Fang is very beautiful."

Johanna turned abruptly. "I'll tell Jaufre," she said over her shoulder, "and then I'm going to Edyk's."

Shasha thought before speaking this time, and then said, very carefully, "Is that wise?"

"Perhaps not," Johanna said, pausing in the doorway. "But it is only fair."

With a lithe, confident stride she was gone, leaving Shasha to reflect ruefully on the wisdom of tying her future to someone as proud and as stubborn and as reckless as Johanna.

But then what could one expect of a child born beneath the broom star? The signs had been there the night of Johanna's birth for all to read. Did the appearance of that cloud banner, that peacock feather in the skies over Everything Under the Heavens not signify the wiping out of the old and the establishment of the new? Certainly the description fit Johanna who, raised by a liberal and loving father, never bothered with the traditional limitations placed on the behavior of females, or children for that matter.

Shasha chuckled. Wu's widow would—and had—taken the legend of the broom star even further, to anticipate drought, famine and disease as a natural consequence of Johanna's birth and continued presence in Wu Li's house. Wu Li had put up with much from his second wife but he had stopped that nastiness in its tracks, so firmly that the second wife had never referred to Johanna again in his presence. If she could not speak ill of the girl, she would not speak of her at all.

Shasha swept up the rubies in her hands and smiled to herself. At least life on the road with Johanna would never be dull.

She thought of Jaufre, and her smile faded. No, not dull at all.

Jaufre had been moved from the house to the stables at the same time Shasha had been moved from the family quarters to the kitchen. He was seated now on a leather folding stool outside his room, coaxing another year's use out of a worn bridle.

"I've just come from a royal audience," she said. "Wu Li's widow has finally seen fit to inform me of my father's death."

"Twenty-four hours after the fact," Jaufre said. His hands stilled and his eyes lifted to hers. "It was better this way, Johanna," he said. "After the accident, it was only a matter of time. Wu Li was not the man to live without his legs."

She turned her face into an errant ray of sunshine and closed her eyes against the glare. "I know. It's just…"

His hand, hard and warm and slightly sweaty, raised to her cheek. "I know."

She pressed her face into his palm. He allowed it for a moment, and then pulled away to resume work on the bridle.

She pulled out a wisp of hay and chewed it, watching him work. He was as unnaturally tall as she, with smooth, tanned skin and startlingly light hair, the first and still the only golden hair she had ever seen, even on the Road. It was thick and clipped short and in the sun gleamed like a polished helmet. His eyes were blue, too, but much darker, like the sky after sunset. He was muscular and agile from work with the bow and the staff and with the horses and hawks and the soft boxing he practiced daily in the garden, taught him by Deshi the Scout since Jaufre had first joined the Wu household. When Johanna had expressed an interest Deshi the Scout had begun teaching her, too.

After Deshi's death, they continued to practice, rising at dawn every morning. After Shu Ming's death, they had both found comfort in the ritual. After Wu Li's remarriage, they had done so under the occasional eye of the second wife's personal guard. He seemed amused. Once Jaufre had said beneath his breath, "I wonder, does he know what happens when we speed this up?"

"Let's not show him," Johanna said with her voice barely above a whisper. "Let's...keep it in reserve."

She made no mention of the way Gokudo sometimes looked at her, of how uncomfortable his presence made her feel. Even on the Road, before the eyes of hundreds of strangers, never had she felt so threatened. She was determined that the widow's bodyguard would have no prior knowledge of just how well the widow's husband's daughter could protect herself at need.

Jaufre looked up to see her eyes fixed on some distant thought, and allowed himself the rare pleasure of a long, unguarded look. A late ray of sun kissed her cheek to gold, and threw her profile into proud relief, the straight nose, the high, shadowed cheekbones, the full lips that curled upwards at their corners, the chin that was somehow delicate and determined at the same time. His eyes strayed to the rich bronze braid of hair, the curls that slipped from their braid to cup her cheeks, coil over her shoulders and around the promising swell of her breasts. Her waist was narrow, her hips slim but rounded, flowing into the long, smooth length of her legs sprawling negligently beside his in the hay.

She was a woman now, not the child she had been when she had convinced him to join his fortunes with the honorable house of Wu. He closed his eyes, took a deep and he hoped unobtrusive breath, and focused once more on the bridle.

Her voice disturbed his thoughts. "Jaufre?"

"What?"

"Your father was a Frankish Crusader," she said.

He shrugged. "So he said. He left his crusade to ride as a caravan guard. Not a very good one, obviously, or our caravan wouldn't have been slaughtered to the last man by Persian bandits."

He spoke without bitterness, but she remembered the lonely, unmarked mound they had left behind, sand heaped by hand as high as he could make it, grains already shifting with the wind. "And your mother was Greek?"

His hands stilled on the bridle. "Yes. Why?"

"All the Greeks I've met are dark," she said. "Was your father fair-haired, as you are?"

He nodded, still working on the bridle. "He said that where he came from, some island to the west, many people have fair hair."

"It is very beautiful."

He grinned, and two deep dimples creased his cheeks. "So all the ladies tell me." She threw a handful of straw at him and he ducked, laughing. "Why so many questions today? You know all you need to know about me."

The full lips curved slightly. "Perhaps."

He resumed work on the bridle. "So. When do we go?"

"Three days from now."

"After the ceremonies for Wu Li."

"Yes."

"Where?"

"We could go first to Khuree," she said tentatively, as if she already knew it was a bad idea.

Jaufre shook his head. "That's the last place we want to go. You are the granddaughter of Marco Polo, Johanna. If the Khan learns that we are traveling west he will turn us into official envoys."

"But he might give us a paiza, as he did my grandfather and his father and uncle. We would have safe conduct anywhere in the world."

"Yes, he might, in fact he probably would, and then we would be bound to his service. He would load us down with missives to the Christian Pope and to all the kings in the West. There would be no time for our own business in the middle of all that tedious diplomacy." He made a disgusted sound. "You've seen them at court, all twittering out of the sides of their mouths, no one meaning a word they say. No, I thank you."

She hid a smile.

"And then we would have to return." He looked at her. "We're not coming back, are we?"

"No," Johanna said. "No, we are not."

"So. Does the widow know we are leaving?"

"No," Johanna said.

He looked at her. "You can hate her, if you want to, Johanna. She deserves your hatred."

"There is something else," she said, missing the grim certainty of his last words.

Before she could tell him what, there was movement at the stable door, and they looked up to see Gokudo watching them, one hand tucked into the wide sash he wore around his waist. It was as black as his topknot of hair, as black as the padded armor he wore at all times, as black as the ebony shaft of the tall spear he invariably carried. The curved point of the steel blade set into the top of the spear reflected the sunlight in a blaze that could hurt the eyes, did one look at it too closely.

Johanna found herself on her feet, Jaufre at her side. A distant part of her mind noticed that they had all three assumed the same stance, shoulders braced, body weight over spread feet, knees slightly bent. Jaufre's hand settled on the hilt of the dagger at his waist. Her own hands hung loosely at her sides, ready for the knives strapped to her forearms to drop into her hands.

Tension sang in the air, until a horse whinnied loudly and thumped his stall.

Gokudo laughed suddenly, a deep, rolling belly laugh that filled the room. "Ha, my young friends," he said in his heavily accented Mandarin. "You are alert. That speaks well for the security of the honorable House of Wu."

Jaufre gave a curt nod. "Did you wish for a horse, Gokudo?"

"I did not, young Jaufre, not at present." The guard gave an airy wave. "Just out for a stroll about the premises." He smiled. He had very white, very even teeth. "All must be in order for the festivities."

Jaufre felt Johanna tense next to him and said smoothly, "Surely you meant the ceremonies, Gokudo."

Gokudo's smile faded. "Surely, I did," he said gently. "Anything else would have been an insult to the memory of the Honorable Wu Li, and an affront to his descendants."

His gaze lingered on Johanna's artificially still face, before it slid slowly and deliberately down the length of her body. He held his gaze for just long enough to offend but not quite long enough to incite, before stepping past them to enter Jaufre's room without invitation. It was small and spare, a cot, a table, an oil lamp, a small chest for clothes. The only decoration was a large sword hanging from the wall, its encrusted hilt older than the leather scabbard it was encased in.

Again without invitation, Gokudo took down the sword and pulled it free. "Eh, Damascus steel." He looked down the blade, first one side and then the other. He pulled back a sleeve, licked his arm and ran the edge of the sword down his skin. "A fine edge, too," he said, inspecting the fine black hairs on the blade and the smooth, unblemished patch of skin it had left behind. "However did you come by such a thing, young Jaufre?"

Ignoring the implied insult, Jaufre said evenly, "It was my father's."

"Ah." Gokudo contemplated the blade, and its scabbard. "You don't use it."

"No."

"A pity." He walked past them into the yard, there to toss the sword into the air and catch it by the hilt as it fell again. "What balance," he said, admiring. "Obviously created by the hand of a master smith." He tossed it into the air again.

Jaufre stepped in front of it to catch it this time. The smack of hilt into hand shouted "Mine!" to anyone within earshot.

When he turned Gokudo was watching him with an assessing eye. "I, too, own a sword, young Jaufre. Perhaps they should meet." He smiled again. He smiled a lot. "In practice, of course."

"Of course," Jaufre said.

Gokudo saluted him, tucked his hands back into his sash, and walked to the house with his usual jaunty step.

Jaufre watched him go, his eyes narrowed. "I wonder how much he heard."

"Nothing," Johanna said. "We were almost whispering."

He looked at her. "He was marking territory, Johanna."

"I noticed," Johanna said with mild sarcasm. "You can't fight him, Jaufre."

He doesn't want to fight me, Jaufre thought. He wants to kill me. "I know," he said. And he thought he knew why.

"Buy time," she said. "It's only three days."

"How?"

"Ask him for lessons with the sword," she said.

"Not from him," Jaufre said. "Never from him. He wears the black armor."

She shrugged. "All Cipangu mercenaries wear black armor."

He looked down at her, a faint smile lightening his expression. "And all Cipangu mercenaries are samurai. Which means they are very, very good at their craft."

"You're afraid of him," she said, not quite a question.

He gave her an incredulous look. "You aren't?" She raised an eyebrow. "Johanna, they say he can take two heads at once with that spear of his."

"They don't say it, he does," she said. "A tale told to frighten children."

"And I'm one of the children?"

She almost apologized before she saw the raised eyebrow, and laughed. "Stop trying to pick a fight."

His own smile faded. "Don't ever turn your back on Gokudo. He could kill us both without a thought and go in to enjoy his breakfast afterward. And he is the widow's creature, through and through."

"Her lover, too," she said, her voice flat.

He turned, surprised. "I didn't know you knew."

"The only person in this house who didn't know was my father," she said.

"If you kill her, we won't live to leave Everything Under the Heavens."

"It is the only reason she is still living," Johanna said, her expression bleak.

He was relieved to hear it, but there was no harm in driving the lesson home. "Well, that, and the fact that her personal guard is an ex-samurai."

She shrugged. "A thug, merely."

"For someone who has spent so much time in Cipangu, you are remarkably ignorant of its culture," Jaufre said with a deadly calm that finally pierced her insouciance. "Samurai are highly trained warriors, educated not just in personal arms but in strategy and tactics as well. This is a man who could not only take off our heads with one swipe of that pig-sticker of his, he could also organize the invasion of Kinsai."

"If he's so great, what is he doing a thousand leagues from home?"

"I don't know," Jaufre said. "He could have offended one of the shogun. He could have been on the losing side of a war." He shrugged. "He could be a spy, sent to Cambaluc to send home information on the stability of the Khan's court. Although I don't think so."

"Why not?"

"Spies, good spies, fade into the background. Gokudo? Likes to put on a show."

She watched Gokudo as he moved across the courtyard. Gokudo, who strutted rather than walked everywhere he went. He held his naginata, sharp, polished, as a badge of office. As a deadly threat.

She looked at the sword Jaufre held. "Maybe you should get in a few lessons with that thing. We should be ready to fight."

"Only if we can't run," he said. "And you know I prefer the bow."

Gokudo reached the front door of the house and went inside, the shadowed interior seeming to swallow his black figure whole.

"Jaufre?"

"What?" he said, going back inside to resheathe and rehang his father's sword on the wall of his room.

"Edyk has offered for me, something my father's widow undoubtedly refers to as a miracle sent from the Son of Heaven himself, as she is now busily planning my marriage."

His hands stilled on the sword but he didn't look around. "He loves you."

"He thinks he does."

"He loves you," Jaufre repeated.

"It doesn't matter," she said. "It wouldn't work. He wouldn't be happy." She paused. "I wouldn't be happy, to stay here in Cambaluc."

"You're sure?"

"I'm sure," she said firmly, and the hard, painful knot in his gut that had been twisting steadily tighter relaxed a little, not much, but enough to let him turn and face her, mask in place. "Besides," she added, with her sudden smile, "we have places to go, you and I and Shasha."

"Money?"

"We have enough. More than enough. Father made sure of that. Shasha will show you. And we can always earn our way. You're a soldier and a caravan master. Shasha's a cook and a healer. And you said yourself I'm as good a horseman and falconer as any you've ever seen, and if worst comes to worst, we can always sing for our suppers." She grinned. "And I know I'm a better diver, even if you won't admit it."

"Cipangu again," he said, a reminiscent smile pulling up one corner of his mouth.

"I brought back more of the rose pearls than you did," she said, with an impish, sidelong glance.

"Only because the fish charmer failed to keep a shark from the diving ground and the rest of us had brains enough to get out of the water," he replied promptly.

"Until you dived in to pull me out. I think you were more afraid of my bringing back more pearls than you had, than you were afraid that I might be eaten by the shark."

He remembered that Gokudo was from Cipangu, and good memories were swamped by a return flood of recent events. He stooped to pick up the bridle he had been working on before Gokudo had come in on them. "And Edyk?"

Her smile vanished as quickly as it had come. "I'm going to see him now. To say goodbye."

He heard the thud of his blood in his ears. The knot in his gut was back, tied more tightly than it had ever been before. His eyes cleared and he saw that the bridle had snapped in two in his hands.

"Jaufre?" she said. "Is something wrong?"

He stood up abruptly and tossed the pieces of bridle into the scrap barrel. When he turned to where she could see his face again it had resumed its usual genial mask. "I'll saddle the Shrimp."

And he did, and he tossed her into the saddle, and he waved her off with a smile, although it was more of a rictus. Shu Shao came out to stand beside him as Johanna kicked the sedate Shrimp into a jolting trot and passed through the wooden gates. "She's off to see Edyk, then?"

He nodded, not trusting his voice to speech.

She nodded. "I'm to show you something."

He followed her into the house, where she produced the rubies of

Mien from her sewing basket. "We are to sew these into the hems of our clothes."

"As Shu Ming said her father did," he said.

She nodded. They were both speaking in whispers, and Shasha had left the door wide open so that they might hear if anyone approached. He leaned in and said, "Shasha, do you know?"

She looked wary. "Know what?"

He took a deep breath. "How Wu Li truly died?"

She cast a quick glance through the door. "Which time?" she said.

He was startled into normal speech, quickly shushed by a gesture. "He didn't fall from his horse, Shasha," he said, his voice low again. "His cinch was cut nearly through."

She was silent for a long moment. "A pity the fall didn't kill him," she said at last.

"Shasha!"

She looked at him, her expression heavy with the burden of knowledge. "A pity the fall didn't kill him," she repeated.

"Why?" But he was afraid he already knew.

"Because," she said, "then the widow would not have dispatched Gokudo to finish the job with Wu Li's own pillow."

He went white. "Shasha. Are you sure?"

"He fought," she said distantly. "I saw blood beneath his fingernails. Before she had me removed from his room, of course."

Following his accident Wu Li had been left without the use of his legs, and there were other, internal injuries at which the learned doctors summoned from the city could only speculate. Now he wondered just how learned those doctors were, and how much the widow Wu had paid them to say what she wanted Wu's household to hear. "Is there no one we can tell? No one to whom we can appeal for justice?"

"Who?" Shasha said simply.

Jaufre cast around for a name. "Ogodei?" he said. "He's a baron of a hundred thousand now. He was a friend to Wu Li."

"And with his promotion he was posted to the west," she said. "He was the first person I thought of. No, Jaufre. There is no one else that I can think of. Wu Li spent just enough time and money at court to keep his business free of their interference. He did not cultivate the kind of friendships we would need to make an accusation against the widow."

They stood in miserable silence before sounds came from the kitchen of the beginnings of dinner.

Shasha gave him a little push toward the door.

"Johanna can't know, Shasha," he heard himself say.

"No," Shasha said grimly. "She most certainly can't."

# · Eight ·

—

Johanna slid down from the Shrimp's back, patting her heaving sides. Patiently she lifted the mare's right front hoof and dug out an offending piece of rock that had become wedged in her hoof. The Shrimp rewarded her efforts by leaning her entire weight on her back.

"You," Johanna said, "are an ungrateful wretch and you should have been turned into fertilizer years ago." She jabbed the horse's belly with an elbow and the Shrimp huffed out an indignant breath and shifted her weight enough for Johanna to finish the task.

Johanna let the Shrimp's hoof fall, and straightened, stretching.

Beneath her Cambaluc stretched on forever, its many rooftops glittering in the afternoon sun, the palace of the Great Khan bulking large to overshadow its neighbors. Johanna stood still, looking her fill. In her expression was appreciation for the beauty of the great city, and respect for the industry and achievement of its citizens, but there was no affection, no pride of place, and none of the sorrow one might expect from one anticipating a permanent exile.

Chiang, Edyk's manservant, answered her knock and bowed her into the house at once. Hearing her voice Edyk jumped up with a glad smile and held out both hands. "Johanna!"

Johanna waited for Chiang, loitering next to the door with a carefully disinterested look on his face, to leave the room. When he at last he did, with a reluctant, backwards glance, she said without preamble, "My father's widow tells me you have offered to marry me."

Edyk's welcoming smile changed to a frown and his hands dropped.

He looked at her searchingly. "The offer was made to your father last year. He told me it was for you to decide, but that in any case I must wait until you were older. He didn't tell you?"

The breath went out of her on a long sigh and she shook her head. "No. No, he wouldn't. He wouldn't want to pressure me, and he knew his second wife and I were not...close."

He touched her shoulder, a gentle, comforting touch. "I know."

She reached up to caress his hand lightly. His arms went out but before he could embrace her she stepped away. "I have come here to explain why I must refuse, Edyk."

He stood very still, his breath caught in his throat, even his heart seemed to cease beating. Jaufre could have told him that Johanna always had that effect on the men in her life, but it had been a long time since Edyk had been willing to listen to anything Jaufre might have to say about Johanna. "What?" someone said, and Edyk realized the stranger's voice was his own. "Johanna, what did you say?" He started forward.

She held up one hand, palm towards him. "Don't! Don't touch me, not yet. Listen. Listen to me, please, Edyk." She stretched out a hand to slide a rice paper door to one side. The plum trees in the garden beyond were flowering and the aroma of their blossoms slipped into the room, curling into every corner, pervasive and bittersweet. Edyk would never be able to smell a plum blossom again without remembering this moment.

Her back to him, Johanna said in a steady voice, "I can't marry you, Edyk. It would be impossible. For both of us."

Now his voice was hard and angry, with an undercurrent of fear. "That's nonsense and you know it. We've grown up side by side, we were friends before we ever, well, you know. Before."

She almost smiled at his stutter over how their relationship had changed. "I know."

"And," he added, "we're both foreigners, in a land that is determined to keep us that way."

"My father was as Chinese as the Son of Heaven himself," she said, an edge to her voice.

"But your mother was half Chinese and half Venetian," he said flatly, "the same as mine is Chinese and Portuguese. Look in your mirror. The Venetian won out. It doesn't matter that we were born here. We are strangers in a strange land, as Bishop John taught us from the book of the Christian god. And we always will be."

"No," she said carefully, back in control. "I won't be. At least I won't be a stranger in this land."

"What do you mean?"

"I mean that I'm leaving, Edyk."

"What?"

She closed her eyes and inhaled the scent of the blossoms. "I'm leaving Cambaluc, Edyk, and Everything Under the Heavens."

"What!" He was really frightened now. He jerked her around to face him. "You're leaving? You're leaving me?"

"Yes."

"To go where? And why?"

"Perhaps," she said, considering, "perhaps I will look for my grandfather."

He snorted. "He's been gone, how long now, thirty years? You never met him, you don't know him. He may be dead, he most likely is, and then where will you be? And even if he is alive, what makes you think he'd want anything to do with you, when he never bothered to stay in contact with his own daughter, your mother?"

"Edyk," she said, her expression relaxing a little. "Have you never wanted to get up of a morning and start walking west?"

He looked at her, a veteran of trading trips north, south, east and, yes, west, and raised an eyebrow.

"All right," she said. "But have you never wished to keep going, to follow the sun to where it sets? To see the fountains of fire in Georgiana? To visit the enchanters of Tebet? To fight the dragons at the edge of the ocean?" The sadness in her eyes faded, to be replaced by excitement and anticipation. It was a look Edyk had seen before, and did not rejoice in now.

She waited, part of her hoping he would agree with her, part of her hoping he would offer to dower his wives and children, sell his business and come with them on the road. When he didn't, she sighed, although it didn't hurt as much as she had imagined it would. "It doesn't matter if my grandfather is alive or dead, Edyk. He is merely an excuse to start me on my way. You know me." She smiled. "You know me better than almost anyone else. Would you expect anything less?"

He took a hasty step away from her, and then back. "And who will take care of you?"

"I can take care of myself," she said.

Edyk could not honestly quarrel with her superb if arrogant self-confidence. Neither was he ready to acknowledge defeat. "You know what the roads are becoming, now that the Great Khan is dead."

"Shasha and Jaufre will be with me."

"Jaufre!" he exclaimed. "Jaufre is going with you?"

"Yes."

"I might have known," he said bitterly.

Johanna looked surprised. "Certainly you might have known," she agreed. "We grew up here together, children of foreigners. We have suffered the shunning of the people of the Son of Heaven all our lives. He wants to leave as badly as I do, and unlike you he is free to do so. And he is my best and oldest friend."

"Johanna." He took both her hands in his and held them tightly. "I know I've never said the words, but I thought you knew. I love you, Johanna. I want to marry you. I want to spend the rest of my life with you. Don't leave me here all alone."

The sadness in her eyes was displaced again, this time by laughter. "And what would Blossom and Jade have to say to that?"

"But they love you!" he protested. "They always have."

"As your friend, yes," she said. "As a third wife?" She shook her head, and the corners of her mouth quirked upwards.

Watching the generous curve of her lips he felt again that sharp, fierce tug of desire, and this time he let it show in his eyes. "Is it the bride price?" he said roughly. "I'll double it. Triple it, even."

She shook her head. "I don't want to be bought," she said gently. "And Edyk, you know you don't want to buy me."

"Then come to me freely," he said. "Come to me naked, I don't care. I want you for my wife, Johanna."

She shook her head again, a final, negating movement.

He recognized the signs. Johanna had a kind of determined, implacable ruthlessness Edyk had never before encountered in a woman. In Johanna's world, there were the people she cared for, and then there was everyone else, worthy of curiosity, certainly, perhaps even of courtesy.... perhaps. The people she cared for—he totted them up mentally and even before one was dead could fit them all on the fingers of one hand—were worthy of any sacrifice, mental, emotional, physical.

There has never been such a woman, he thought, looking at the gallant chin, the squared shoulders, the bronzed hair escaping its braid to curl riotously around her face, the eyes the color of the sky over Kesmur just before dawn. He let his eyes drift down her body, over the swell of her breasts, the indentation of her waist, the long legs. "But I want you," he said at last, hazarding his all in a voice gone thick with need. "Johanna, I want you."

"Then take me," she said huskily. His eyes met hers and he felt a shock of recognition at the desire he saw reflected there. "I want you, too. I need you. And I want something for myself. Something for my very own, to take away with me, to keep me warm on the long dark nights away from you." He was frozen with disbelief and she took a step forward and caught at his hand. "Edyk, please," she said, and raised his hand to her breast. "Please love me."

He felt the rich weight of her breast, the nipple already hard beneath the palm of his hand, and pulled her into his arms, bringing his mouth down on hers so roughly her lip split. He tasted blood and lifted his head to see her eyes half-closed, her skin flushed, her lips parted. Her tongue came out to touch the cut, and with a groan he was unable to suppress cradled himself between her thighs, sliding his hands over her bottom to lift and rub her against him. She responded, eagerly if inexpertly, and such was his instantaneous need that he would have taken her then and there, on the floor, if she had not called to him in a voice soft and shaken with desire. "Edyk, Edyk, not here. Not here," she repeated when he raised his head again, dazed, almost uncomprehending. She smoothed his hair back with one trembling hand. "Anyone could come in."

He pulled away from her. "Where, then?" he demanded, unsmiling, the planes of his face hard and strained.

"The lake. The summerhouse. We will be alone there."

He looked at her, his eyes burning, his mouth compressed. "The summerhouse is two hours from here, Johanna."

She smiled at him, a rich, bewitching smile of shared desire that promised him everything she had to give and more. "Then we'd better get started, hadn't we?"

At her smile his body responded promptly and he cursed her. She laughed. He flung open the door and bellowed for Chiang, who appeared almost immediately, still with that carefully nurtured expression of disinterest. "Saddle North Wind," Edyk snapped, and turned back to Johanna.

She was still laughing. "North Wind?" she said. "You actually ride North Wind?"

"He's the fastest horse in my stables and he doesn't race again until next week," he said grimly.

Her smile was provocative. "And he lets you ride him?"

"He will if you're with me." And indeed when Chiang brought the horse around from the stables he caught Johanna's scent and whinnied eagerly, almost trotting with Chiang dangling at the end of his reins. He almost danced to a stop and nosed eagerly at the front of her tunic. She laughed and fed him a piece of carrot and rubbed his ears.

""I should never have let you near him as a colt," Edyk said grimly. He threw Johanna up into the saddle without ceremony, yanked the reins from Chiang and vaulted up after her.

"The Shrimp!" Johanna said protestingly.

"The Shrimp! Great Khan! You rode the Shrimp up here? I'm surprised either of you finished the trip alive." He pulled her back against him, and heard her gasp. "Yes," he said with satisfaction. "You want to go to the summerhouse, fine, but we'll ride the Wind there together, Johanna." He kicked the white stallion into a canter. North Wind, a horse with a mind of his own, thought it should be a gallop and Edyk was only too willing to oblige.

All the same, it was the longest, most torturous journey Edyk the Portuguese, veteran of many crossings of the Taklamakan Desert, was ever to make. Once out of the city the road narrowed to a rough trail and became steep and rocky. North Wind of necessity slowed to a walk. Johanna leaned back in the cradle of Edyk's arms, her body rubbing against his with the Wind's every step. By the time they reached the lake, hidden at the head of a small valley south of Cambaluc, Edyk was frantic with the need to get at her, to lay her skin bare to his eyes and his touch.

Johanna was no less frantic to let him. All the long way up to the lake, Edyk's hands and lips were never still, and his voice, husky with desire, had whispered in between kisses and bites exactly what he was going to do to her, and how. When his feet hit the ground she hurled herself forward into his arms, almost knocking him over. She could feel him press into her belly and she rubbed up against him, moaning.

He slid his hands over her hips and held her still. He let his head fall back and drew a great rush of air into his lungs, holding it, and then letting it expel from his chest in an explosive rush. "Johanna, wait," he said. Loving had always been enjoyable for him, sweet, a mutually-pleasing frolic. With Johanna the pleasure was so intense it was almost pain, a demon that had him by the scruff of the neck who wouldn't let go until he had satisfied it, and he knew he must slow himself down or he would hurt her. He clenched his teeth and made an effort to speak intelligibly. "This is your first time, isn't it?"

"You know it is," she muttered, licking at the drop of sweat that had collected in the hollow of his throat, sliding her hands down his back to pull him tightly against her. He caught her hands and she made a frustrated sound and tried to pull free. "I want to touch you, Edyk. Let me."

He raised her chin with one hand and looked into the clear eyes that were now dark with thwarted desire. "I want to let you," he said softly. "But I'm all sweaty from the ride, and so are you. Let's swim first."

"I don't want to swim," she said crossly, urging him forward again.

He gave a laugh that turned into a shaken groan. Again he caught her hands and said with difficulty, "Stop that. I don't want to swim either, but we have to slow this down a little." He looked into her eyes and whispered, "Trust me to do this right, Johanna."

She closed her eyes tightly for a moment. When she opened them again the desire was still there but on a leash. "All right," she said. "What do you want me to do?"

He pulled her towards the lake. "We have to take off our clothes to swim, don't we?"

She brightened, marched down to the water's edge and without further ado pulled her tunic over her head. The setting sun played over her flushed skin, gilding her nipples. Her trousers followed her tunic and the sun turned the soft curls between her long legs to gold. The sight nearly drove him to his knees. "Johanna," he said, his throat thick. "You're as beautiful as I thought you would be. No. More beautiful than I ever dreamed."

She reached for him with impatient hands, pulling his tunic over his head, finding the ties of his trousers and slipping them down. She stood back to look at him, from dark eyes to wide shoulders to strong arms to narrow hips to sturdy legs and back up to rampant, strutting desire. "So are you."

She stretched out a hand to touch him. He grabbed it and used it to lead her into the lake. The water was lukewarm, but to their overheated skins still a shock. They cupped it in trembling hands and smoothed it over their bodies. Johanna leaned forward to follow her hands with her lips, sipping the water from his skin from mouth to chest to thigh, to touch her tongue to the length of flesh upright and hot and hard against his belly.

He pulled her out of the lake and into his arms. Her skin, cool from the water, shivered delightfully against his and he bent his head and placed his lips to her breast. One hand knotted in her hair, the other slipped between her legs to find her wet and hot, and with a groan he kissed his way down her body to bury his mouth in her. She cried out her pleasure, back arching like a bow, and would have fallen but for his arms steadying her.

"Johanna, Johanna," he muttered against the soft skin of her belly. "I'm sorry, I can't wait any longer."

"Finally." He almost laughed at the breathless exasperation in her voice, and forgot to when she slid to her knees, her mouth seeking out his, her hands exploring. "Please, Edyk," she sobbed, clutching at his shoulders. "Please."

"All right," he said through gritted teeth, and pulled her down on him, so that for the first time she felt all that heat and pride pressed up inside her. If there was pain she never felt it. She came to climax at once, crying out in sheer delight, opening her eyes afterwards to see him staring at her, his eyes burning, his body still hard within her, and then she felt the cool grass against her spine as he laid her down.

He brushed the hair back from her face, kissed her, tiny, teasing kisses, holding himself inside her as the sweet shuddering of her body slackened. Then he began to move, long, deep strokes, pushing slowly all the way up, then pulling as slowly out, loitering both within her heated flesh and without, teasing her, taunting her, urging her on to renewed desire. She gasped at the return of feeling, staring up at him with wide astonished eyes and parted lips. He smiled. Her hips began to lift to his and he threw back his head. "Yes." When he drew almost all the way out she dug her nails into his back in protest and her inner muscles closed around him. He groaned and began thrusting faster and harder and deeper. She wrapped her legs around him and met him thrust for thrust. When he plunged inside her for the last time she convulsed and cried out, a low, disbelieving sound joined to his own growled pleasure.

They lay speechless in the light of the rising moon for a long time afterward. When he had recovered he shifted his weight. Wordlessly she clutched him to her, silently protesting, and he subsided, content to remain where he most longed to be.

Presently she stirred, and he raised his head to see her eyes sparkling in her flushed face, tendrils of hair clinging to her skin, her braid damp and tangled against her neck. In a voice lazy with pleasure she observed, "Now I know what Jade and Blossom have been giggling about for the last three years."

"What!"

She said reasonably, "Well, we had to talk about something, and they can't ride and I don't embroider, and all we had in common was you."

He stared at her for a long, long moment. She grinned, and he threw back his head and shouted with laughter. She laughed with him, and the sound of it pealed across the still water of the lake and lingered beneath the boughs of the drooping willow trees.

Thinking of it afterwards, he supposed they must have eaten and slept, but all he could remember was the laughter and the loving, on the floor, in the grass, in the lake, sometimes they even made it as far as the bed. She gave him everything her smile had promised and more. His thoughts, his hands, the strands of his hair, the pores of his skin, his nostrils were filled with the taste and texture and smell of her. He memorized the straight, arrogant bridge of her nose, the sultry curve of her mouth, the vulnerable hollow of her throat, the sweet slope of her breast, the silken texture of her skin, the seductive smell of her femininity. She responded completely, openly, wholeheartedly, without reservation or shyness, her astonished pleasure at each new sensual delight a reward in itself. He taught her the difference between loving and rutting, he seduced her sweetly and showed her how to return in kind, every skill he had learned from every woman he had ever loved he exerted to show her how much he cared, how much he needed, how much he wanted this one woman in his arms, in his life.

He could not bear to think of life without her, and so he didn't think of it. "We will build a home in Kinsai," he murmured into her hair late into their second night at the summerhouse. "We will have many sons, and we will teach them to bargain and to trade, and take them with us when we travel. I love you, Johanna."

"I love you, Edyk," she whispered.

His last thought before he fell into a deep, dreamless sleep with her locked securely in his arms was, she'll never leave me now.

But when he woke the next morning, she was gone.

So was North Wind.

# · Nine ·

⊢——⊣

Norstate Wind was not the only priceless possession to have gone
missing in Cambaluc that morning.

The house of the late, honorable Wu Li was in an uproar as his
widow stormed through every room, leaving chaos in her wake. Drawers
were yanked out, their contents dumped on the floor, the drawers tossed
aside. Shiny lacquered boxes were wrenched open, found wanting, and
hurled against the wall. Tall porcelain vases were turned upside down
and shaken in vain for anything that might have been secreted there, and
when they proved empty were shattered into a hundred pieces on every
hearthstone.

"Where are they?" the widow said. Her voice rose to a shriek. "Where
are they!"

The kitchen was a scene of bedlam by the time she finished there. The
undercook bled from four parallel scratches on his cheek from the widow's
nails. Every pot was taken from its hook, every pan from its shelf, the spit
pulled from the wall and used as a club to strike the drab assigned to turn
it. The drab lay unconscious in a corner, breathing stertorously through
bubbles of blood that extended and retracted through her nostrils. One
of the maids was blinded, possibly permanently, having caught the brunt
of the widow's rings across her eyes. The rest of the servants had fled, or
were cowering beneath tables and chairs and behind doors and bureaus,
hoping against hope to escape her notice.

Gokudo was made of sterner stuff. "My lady," he said.

She snarled and whirled, both hands curled into bejeweled claws.

"Where are they?" she shouted, advancing on him.

"I do not know, my lady," he said.

She raised a hand, long, now broken fingernails already stained with blood. "Tell me where they are! The stables!" She stepped forward. "Get out of my way!"

Gokudo stood his ground. "Wu Li's daughter is gone," he said.

She didn't appear to hear him, at first, the mad light in her eyes undiminished, the claw of a hand still upraised to strike. He repeated himself, raising his voice, enunciating each word in a slow, clear voice. "The daughter of the honorable Wu Li is gone from this house. As is Shu Shao, the kitchen drudge, and Jaufre, the stable boy."

This time she heard him.

They stood there, facing each other, motionless, no sound in the kitchen except for the heavy breathing of the widow, the whimpers of the undercook, and the crackle of a cinder, raked out from the hearth in the struggle over the spit and now doing its best to set fire to the floor.

Her hand dropped. "Show me," she said.

It was the first time she had been in the little mongrel's room. The smallness of the room, the shabbiness of its furnishings did not register with her.

What did register was the narrow bed, neatly made, and the box resting in the middle of the plumped pillow with the carefully mitered corners. Clad in layers of black lacquer, scarlet leaves twined around the join between lid and base, the box was in itself a work of art a handspan square. It had been made for its purpose, and it looked well used, and well loved.

Wu Li's widow had no thought for the craftsmanship of the thing. She snatched it up and tugged. The lid was so well made that the seal created a vacuum that resisted her efforts. She tugged in vain. She even broke another nail. Tears of rage began to course down the widow's painted cheeks, and she flung the box at Gokudo. "Open it!"

Gokudo got his hands up just in time to stop the box from hitting him in the face. He found the catch on the lid, and it opened with a huff of sound, the lid standing up on its intricately hand-crafted brass hinges. He held the box out at arm's length so she could see inside. He could already tell what it contained by its weight.

She remained bent over the box, staring inside it with burning eyes.

There was a commotion at the front of the house. The widow didn't move, and Gokudo swore and went to see what it was.

Edyk the Portuguese was struggling with the door man. "Where is she? Where is North Wind? Where are they? Tell this fool to let me go!"

"Release him, Bo He," Gokudo said.

Bo He, an elderly gentleman in a ruffled state, stepped back and smoothed his coat. "As my mistress wishes," he said.

Gokudo raised his hand to strike him for his insolence, but Edyk the Portuguese stepped forward. "Where is she? Where is Johanna? Is North Wind in your stables? Take me to them at once!"

"We shelter neither your whore nor your nag in this house, Edyk the Portuguese," Gokudo said, not bothering to hide his sneer.

Edyk stopped and stared at him. "Johanna isn't here? Where is she? When do you expect her back?"

Gokudo laughed, and Edyk raised his hand to strike him. Gokudo slapped it to one side and followed up with a sharp blow to Edyk's sternum with the flat of his other hand. Edyk flew backward, tumbling to the ground in the center of the courtyard. He made as if to scramble to his feet and froze with the point of Gokudo's naginata at his throat.

"Get up," Gokudo said contemptuously. "Please, do get up."

Edyk dropped and rolled out out of reach and got back on his feet. He snatched up a hoe someone had let fall in a bed of narcissus during the widow's rampage and dropped into a guard stance, only to have the blade of the naginata slice off the head. Instead of retreating as Gokudo had every right to expect, Edyk thrust with the end of the stick, striking Gokudo hard in the chest. By the time the samurai caught his breath Edyk was gone and the bodyguard could hear the sound of hoofbeats from the other side of the gate, departing rapidly.

He cursed when he got his breath back, loudly and fluently in his native tongue, and spun around to see Bo He watching. He didn't like the expression on the majordomo's face so he cut it off. He stepped over the gurgling remains of the old man's body and went back into the house to find Dai Fang.

She had returned to her own quarters and was in the restored orderliness of her sitting room with a pot of tea steaming in front of her. The madness of her fury was gone, vanished as if it had never been, to be replaced by a cold and deadly intensity that caused a ripple of unease to break out down the back of even his warrior spine.

She poured tea for both of them, and presented his cup with both hands. "Find her," she said.

"My lady—"

She raised her eyes to his. "Find her, and bring her to me."

He did the only thing she would permit. He bowed his head, accepted the tea, and said, "As my lady wishes."

Her voice stopped him at the door. "And Gokudo?"

"My lady?"

Her glittering eyes raised to his. "In what condition she is returned to the home of her father is of no concern to me."

He bowed again, and thought, not for the first time, of the bronze braid wrapped around his fist, and of forcing wide the long, lissome legs of the daughter of the house. "As my lady wishes."

· Part II ·

# · Ten ·

Spring, 1322 A.D.

⊢——⊣

The yambs the Great Khan commanded to be built half a century before that greeted those traveling the road west at every eighth league had yet to fall into disrepair, and the great trees he planted to show the way were just beginning to leaf out as Johanna's tiny group passed between them. Occasionally they met an imperial mailman, hurrying to complete his sixty daily leagues, but for most of the way the road was as bare of company as her companions were bare of conversation.

Jaufre had been curt and uncommunicative since Johanna's return from the summerhouse, riding North Wind. Johanna, rebuffed in her efforts to share her wonderful new feelings of freedom and independence, was bewildered and resentful and surly in turn. Shasha, glancing surreptitiously from one to the other as if to gauge the amount of unvented spleen gathering in each youth, kept her own counsel.

And the glittering roofs of Cambaluc faded in the distance. They followed the road west, stopping at Shensi only to feed and water the horses and find a quick meal for themselves. They traveled well into the night, made a cold camp and were up again before the sun the following morning.

"What's the rush?" Jaufre said finally, and irritably.

Johanna settled the saddle in place, looking over North Wind's back at the road they had come down the day before. "My father's second wife doesn't like being crossed," she said. As if aware that this was a meager explanation for driving them down the road like a slave trader late for an auction, she added, "She will be very angry that she will now not receive the commission on Edyk's marriage settlement." She checked again to see that the clasp on the leather pouch she wore at her waist was secure.

"Wu Li's widow will be delighted to be rid of us," Jaufre said, yanking at a cheek strap so hard that his horse whinnied and danced in reproof. "Three less bellies to fill, three less servants to pay. The heir to Wu Li's estate conveniently missing. I doubt she'll make any effort to come after you."

"Nonetheless, I, too, will rest more easily when we are out of her reach," Shasha said, watching Johanna with a speculative gaze.

Johanna saw Shasha watching her. She flushed and dropped her hand.

"Well, then, perhaps you could just tell us where it is we're going in such a hurry," Jaufre said with awful sarcasm.

Johanna froze up. "I would have thought you would recognize the road," she said, as haughty as a mandarin's mistress.

Shasha beat a strategic retreat and waited for the explosion from a safe distance. She hoped it would be a loud one. With blows, even. Anything to clear the air.

A bright ray of morning sun flooded their campsite with light. Johanna was here, Jaufre thought in sudden realization, here, with him. She had not stayed behind with Edyk. She had turned her back on the security of marriage, a life of ease and comfort, and the affection of a man sure to love her and indulge her all her life long.

She had not chosen that life. Instead, she was traveling the Road west with him, Jaufre. The Road was no refuge, no sanctuary, no safe haven. At every league there was a new and almost invariably fatal disease waiting to infect them, thieves and bandits eager to rob them, rival merchants hoping to cheat them, bears and wolves with their next meal on their minds. There were poisonous snakes and insects and wells poisoned by nature or by man. They could be struck by lightning on the plains, smothered in sand in the desert, buried in snow in the mountains. They could lose their way. They could be deliberately misdirected, and attacked.

But here she was, with him, on that Road. Edyk the Portuguese was a memory back in Cambaluc, and Cambaluc was falling farther behind them every day.

North Wind shied at a dragonfly and pulled at his picket, his white coat gleaming in the dawn light. North Wind, the preeminent race horse of his day and Edyk's pride and joy, now Johanna's saddle horse.

Jaufre burst out laughing. Johanna looked around, startled. Still laughing, he reached out to pull her braid in not quite his old, brotherly manner, but close enough to lay her hackles. Johanna melted instantly, grinning at him, every constraint falling away, not thinking to question why there had been any constraint to begin with.

Shasha muttered to herself. They looked at her. "So we go to Chang'an," she said. "And who do we meet in Chang'an?"

"Guess," Johanna said.

Shasha stared at her with rising suspicion. "Johanna, you wouldn't!"

"I would, too," Johanna said.

Shasha groaned. "Not old No-Nuts!"

"The very same," Johanna said proudly. She moved to tie her bedroll to the back of North Wind's saddle, and added in a reproving voice, "And I don't think that's a very respectful way to refer to my honorable uncle, either."

Jaufre turned his face so that Shasha wouldn't see his grin.

Shasha took a deep breath and swore with a surprising range and fluency.

Johanna widened her eyes and said in a shocked voice, "But, Shasha! I thought you liked Uncle Cheng!" Shasha wasn't finished swearing and Johanna said reproachfully, "Such is gratitude. And after Uncle Cheng rescued your teeth from that prince in Zeilan, too."

"If that idiot hadn't tried to buy off the local priest with pork instead of beef, my teeth wouldn't have been in any danger in the first place," Shasha said tartly.

"Well," Johanna said, vaulting astride North Wind and glancing at the increasing light on the eastern horizon, "the sooner we start the sooner you can abuse him all you like to his face. We've got to hurry. He wrote me that he wants to start no later than the night of the new moon."

"Isn't that tonight?" Jaufre said.

The sound of North Wind's hoofbeats racing away was her reply.

And indeed Wu Cheng was seen to be pacing impatiently up and down in front of the East Gate of Chang'an, alternately kicking and cursing any camel unfortunate enough to get in his way.

Johanna waved. "Uncle Cheng! Uncle Cheng!"

He halted, staring at the three horses galloping in his direction, and then waved back vigorously before turning to shout at the packers. There was a great flurry of movement and the sounds of disgruntled camels spitting and snapping and groaning as they levered themselves up, one half at a time.

"Nice horse," Wu Cheng said when Johanna reined in. If North Wind looked familiar to him, Wu Cheng, an inveterate gambler, possessed the discretion not to say so. He scowled at Shasha. "You had to bring her?"

She grinned. "Of course, Uncle. It wouldn't do for you to be bored on the journey."

The scowl deepened. Unintimidated, Johanna said, "How big is the caravan this year, Uncle? It looks enormous."

The scowl faded. One sure way to divert Wu Cheng was to praise his caravan. "A thousand camels."

Johanna knew her duty and was properly impressed. "Imagine!"

Wu Cheng grinned. "Well, maybe nine hundred, and of course not all my own."

"How many other traders travel with us?"

The scowl came back. "A dozen, so far, and a more useless pack of ninnies I never saw—"

"—in all my days on the Road, and they are many—" Jaufre said.

"—no more idea of the dangers than a newborn babe, and of less use—" Johanna said.

"—and all I'm doing by agreeing to take them into my caravan," said Shasha, unable to resist, "—is inviting disaster down upon all our heads."

Wu Cheng stared, and then threw back his head and laughed, a big, booming noise that turned the heads of everyone in line at the Gate. "Well, well," he said, "it may be that I have guided this caravan before." He cuffed Johanna lightly across the ears. She ducked out of the way, grinning. "Put your horses with the others, then, and find your camels. The girls of Dunhuang, Turpan, and Kashgar are waiting for us!" he bellowed, and there was a ragged cheer from his men. He mounted his camel and it came gruntingly up on all four ungainly legs. Wu Cheng adjusted his seat and squinted at the horizon, alert to a telltale wisp of cloud or column of dust.

Shasha and Jaufre both noticed that while Wu Cheng watched the western horizon, Johanna watched the east. Jaufre thought it was because of Edyk. Shasha did not.

They would both have been surprised. The sun was sinking in a magnificent red-orange blaze, casting a golden shadow over the land. Everything Under the Heavens had never seemed as beautiful to Johanna as it did now, and she discovered to her surprise that there were tears in her eyes.

Goodbye, my father, she thought. Thank you for giving me life. Thank you for giving me my freedom. I love you. I will always love you. And I will live my life to make you proud.

She bowed her head, and Jaufre, riding behind, saw the last ray of the setting sun strike her bronzed hair, and knew he would forgive her anything. He urged his camel to come alongside hers and reached for her hand. She looked up, smiling through her tears, and her hand clasped his in return.

He told himself that it was enough.

For now.

They traveled through the night, eating in the saddle, and did not stop until the sun broke free of the horizon the next morning and the temperature began to rise. They made a dry camp, spreading bedrolls beneath yurts and awnings of light cloth fixed between the camels' saddles and tent poles stuck in the sand. The guards dug latrines. The cooks busied themselves with what would be their main and only hot meal each day. Smoke from the fires curled lazily into a clear, colorless sky slowly darkening to a brassy blue.

The encampment was the size of a small city and indeed resembled one from the top of a dune a short distance away. Clustered at the top of the dune were Uncle Cheng and Johanna's party, mounted again on their horses. North Wind was fidgety and finicky, wanting to stretch his neck into a run. Jaufre's bay gelding was composed and businesslike and disinclined to put up with any of North Wind's nonsense. Shasha rode a flirtatious little gray mare who in movement seemed to dance rather than canter.

"My nephew has joined his ancestors, then," Cheng said.

Johanna let her eyes trace the tops of the tents of their wayfaring village, outlined against the yellow dunes. It was a familiar sight, lacking only the energetic, capable figure of her father. "He has, uncle."

Cheng rested a hand on her knee. "It is better so." His eyes met Jaufre's, and he frowned slightly at the hard expression he saw there.

"I know, uncle," Johanna said. "But—"

"But," he said, nodding, and gave her knee a final pat before sitting erect in the saddle again. He himself was riding a venerable donkey who carried himself and Wu Cheng with something of an air, as if he knew he provided transportation for the leader of their expedition and was determined to lend them both dignity.

Cheng himself bore little resemblance to his nephew, being taller and much heavier. The mandarins and the eunuchs were warring factions at court, with the old khan favoring the eunuchs, and castration was seen as way into power by ambitious parents. Cheng had been offered up for the procedure at the age of ten, and was rewarded with an immediate entrance into the Royal Academy. This was followed by a post at court, where a combination of ability and relative honesty saw his star rise fast and far.

He was among the inner circle of the previous khan, which contributed to his subsequent banishment when the new khan took power and brought in his own eunuchs. He went to Wu Hai, in whose business he had invested most of his own earnings, and Wu Hai put him on the first caravan heading west, which very probably saved his life from the same purge that had taken the life of Johanna's grandmother. He made his home in Chang'an and once it was safe to return to Cambaluc became an infrequent but familiar guest in Wu Li's house. One of Johanna's earliest memories was of sitting on Uncle Cheng's knees during one of his many visits, learning a complicated game of changing patterns played with a knotted round of string.

"Where do you go, then?" Cheng said. He had met Wu Li's second wife. He knew without being told at least one reason why they were leaving Everything Under the Heavens.

"West," Jaufre said.

"Ah," Cheng said. "And how far?"

"Until the ocean drops off the edge of the world, uncle," Johanna said, tears banished now, "and the dragons who live there burn us up with their fiery breath."

Wu Cheng laughed. "As far as that? A very long journey, indeed." He paused. "It is a new and very different world to which you travel, Johanna."

"Yes, and won't it be exciting!" she said. "You know father never traveled beyond Kashgar on our western journeys. I've always wondered what the Pamirs look like from the other side. What an adventure, uncle!"

Her uncle could have said many things in response to this blithe comment, but held his fire, for the moment. "I will be sad to see you go," he said instead. "It is not likely we will meet again on this earth."

"Who is to say?" Johanna said, not wanting to agree but knowing this was most likely true. "We might meet on the Road again one day, honorable uncle."

Wu Cheng smiled. "We might at that, honorable niece."

She felt for the pouch at her waist. Had her father's widow missed them yet? Very likely, and how furious she would be, and how much more so with no abomination of a child to take it out on, and how much more furious than that when she sent out riders and discovered that Johanna was now out of her reach. Johanna contemplated her father's widow's reaction with a great deal of satisfaction.

On her left, Shasha noticed the gesture, and wondered at the unease that whispered up her spine.

Jaufre noticed only the smile pulling at the corner's of Johanna's lips. "You look happy," he said.

She breathed in, deeply. "Do you smell that, Jaufre?"

"What?" He sniffed. "You mean the salt air?"

She shook her head, still smiling. "Freedom," she said.

He thought about it, even as she nudged North Wind into motion. The stifling tension that had infused the house of the honorable Wu Li from the moment he had brought his second wife home. The inchoate threat everyone had felt the day Dai Fang introduced Gokudo. The year full of encroaching snubs and slights as Dai Fang moved Jaufre out of the house and into the stables, Johanna from her suite near the garden to her room off the scullery, Shasha from her position as one of the family to that of a kitchen maid.

The only time they had been able to breathe was on the road with Wu Li. Jaufre had a very clear memory of his own father, but he was long dead and so would Jaufre had been, were it not for Wu Li and Shu Ming and Shasha, and always and ever, Johanna. He knew who his family was.

He nudged his bay into a stride to match North Wind's, at least temporarily. Johanna turned her head to meet his eyes. "Freedom," he said.

"Freedom!" they shouted together, and their horses, in that unexplainable way that horses do divined the high spirits of their riders and moved smoothly into a gallop, kicking up a cloud of dust that hung in the air, obscuring their passing, leaving only an echo of laughter behind.

Until the dust settled again, and left their tracks plain for anyone with the eyes to see.

Heading west. Always and ever, west.

# · Eleven ·

———

When they rose again at dusk, the last trader to join their caravan had arrived, and there was a flurry of packing and loading. When it was done Uncle Cheng called the leader of each merchant group traveling with them into a conference. "I am Wu Cheng. Most of us have traveled together before but for those who are new to me, this is how it goes. We sleep days and travel nights. You are expected to be packed and ready to travel at dusk each day. You care for your own livestock. You buy and cook your own food, and I don't want to be arbitrating any arguments over how you like your rice boiled. If someone gets sick, they will be quarantined until we arrive at the first available town or caravansary. If someone gets hurt to the point that it affects their ability to travel, they will be left at the first available town or caravansary. This caravan is not a traveling hospital."

He let that sink in before going on. "If there is a fire, everyone turns out to fight it, and each morning everyone is responsible for locating the camels carrying the water sacks, which will every morning always be picketed next to the guards' tents, which every morning will always be next to my yurt." He pointed. "The one marked by the red and yellow pennon. Can everyone see it?"

Everyone nodded, very solemn, even those who had heard it many times before. They had to camp closely together for security, which also put everyone and their goods at risk if a fire broke out.

"Fighting, for whatever reason, inclination, drunkenness, gambling or sheer bad temper," Uncle Cheng said. "Not in camp, and see my previous remarks about anyone getting hurt, I don't care whether you started it or not. My plan is to get this caravan to Kashgar in seventy days, before the worst of the summer heat, and anyone who delays us in any way or for any reason will be left behind, willing or unwilling." He tucked his hands in his belt and stared around the circle.

He looked perfectly calm and even relaxed, but Johanna and Jaufre exchanged a knowing glance. Jovial Uncle Cheng could appear quite intimidating at will.

"There are women and children traveling with us. None of them are to be interfered with in any way. If any such interference does occur and the report is credible, the offender will be taken under guard to the nearest city or caravansary and remanded to the custody of the local magistrate, with a recommendation of extreme prejudice." He jerked a thumb at the man standing next to him. "And that's only if my havildar doesn't see fit to deal with the offender first. In which action, whatever it is, he will always have my full authority and support."

Johanna couldn't quite make out the man standing in Uncle Cheng's shadow, who seemed to bow slightly and then efface himself.

"Please don't test us in this. It will not end well for you." Uncle Cheng's smile was thin. "Although it may well end you entirely."

Another uncomfortable silence, broken by a Persian sheik in flowing robes and grizzled beard. "Worthy Wu Cheng, are there reliable reports on the road ahead?"

"Sheik Mohammed," Wu Cheng said with a respectful bow in return. "Are we at risk of attack by bandits, do you mean?"

The sheik inclined his head.

Uncle Cheng stroked his long, thin mustaches. "Well, we are at less risk traveling together simply because there are so many of us. Bandit gangs don't generally tend to attack large numbers. But we've all heard the stories. We must be alert and vigilant, and I beg of you all, urge your people to be discreet. It is well known that the larger bands have agents of their own in some of the larger towns, and they will be looking for easy targets."

"And if we are attacked?" another voice said, this one belonging to the man standing next to the sheik. He was younger and like enough to the sheik to claim him as father.

"We will defend ourselves," Uncle Cheng said. "You all carry arms and know how to use them or I wouldn't have allowed you to join this caravan. Keep your weapons in good working order and within reach. My havildar will instruct you further, one at a time, on this evening's march, but what it boils down to is if we come under attack we bunch up in a group. They will always pick off stragglers. Any pack camel here would be worthy of the effort, especially if they manage to capture any people, who I'm sure I don't have to tell you can be sold as slaves at the greatest possible profit."

He let the words linger on the air for a moment, and then brought his two ham hands together in a loud smack. "We will be traveling fast but there will be time to buy and sell along the way. If a majority of you think we ought to stay an extra day at the market in, say, Kuche, or Yarkent, I will certainly acquiesce to the will of the majority. However, I will expect us to make up the extra day on the road."

He smiled again, more widely, and such was his personal charisma that Johanna felt an immediate lessening of tension around the circle. "I have planned an extra full day's stop at every oasis town we travel through, so if we stay on schedule there will be regular opportunities for rest, refit, and to buy supplies. And for wine, women and song."

There was a ripple of laughter and a relaxation of tension.

"All right," Wu Cheng said briskly. "Mount up."

The first few days of travel was all confusion and vexation. Various groups wishing to travel together jockeyed for position in line and generally succeeded only in embroiling themselves, their animals and surrounding travelers in a hopeless tangle of reins, stirrups and leading strings. They were straightened out again by sweating, swearing handlers and guards, and provided Uncle Cheng with multiple opportunities to demonstrate in six different languages his comprehensive and inspiring command of invective. During one of these instructional episodes Shasha saw Johanna sitting to one side, repeating certain phrases silently. Johanna looked up to see Shasha watching and had the audacity to grin.

On the second day a trader from Balkh managed to mislay ten camels. The rest of the caravan carried on while Uncle Cheng's havildar and a squad of guards were sent out to retrieve them. They returned in the middle of the night, missed in the dark by most of the caravaners, who were treated the following morning to the unpleasant spectacle of a thief and his three co-conspirators stripped to their waists and beaten until their backs were bloody. The missing camels were produced and returned to their grateful owner, who became a shade less grateful when Uncle Cheng assessed two of the camels as payment in full for the retrieval.

The lesson was well taken by everyone watching, but both were unsettling sights for the rest of them to take to their beds that morning. That evening, before the caravan set off again, by Uncle Cheng's express command the four were left to make their way back to Chang'an as best they could, stripped of their shoes and with no water or food to ease their way.

Johanna lingered at the tail end of the caravan, watching the four pitiful figures staggering eastwards.

Unnoticed, Uncle Cheng had ridden up beside her. "Well, niece? Do you judge me to be too harsh?"

She turned to meet his eyes and said without flinching, "No, uncle. I'm just surprised you didn't kill them outright."

The corner of his mouth quirked.

"But then," she said demurely, "there would be no one left alive to attest to the swift and certain justice of that greatest of all caravan masters, the mighty and terrible Wu Cheng."

He burst out laughing. Hearing it, the four felons broke into a staggering run. "Hah! What a caravan master you would have made yourself, honorable niece!"

"And," she said, jerking a thumb over her shoulder at the receding caravan, "none of them will forget it, either. Not the punishment, and certainly not the finder's fee."

He pulled his camel's nose around. "Not from here to Kashgar," he agreed cheerfully. "Serves them right for being so careless of their stock. And it is good to teach a strong lesson early in the trip. It saves much trouble later on."

"Really, uncle," Johanna said drily, "you owe them a debt of gratitude."

"Indeed I do, honorable niece," he said, "and I have paid it. They yet live."

The four would-be thieves toiled up over a dune and dropped out of sight.

There were the usual difficulties between incompatible personalities, tribes and religions, but Uncle Cheng dealt firmly with anything that upset his peace and the peace of the traders traveling under his protection. One hapless Turgesh tripped over a tent pole and fell headlong into a tent full of Muslim women, and only quick footwork prevented a full-blown riot on the part of the women's male relatives. There were the usual rivalries between traders as well, but again Uncle Cheng was quick to take notice and nip anything incendiary in the bud before it had a chance to flower into a fruit that would poison the entire enterprise.

By the time they reached Lanchow, the Golden City, the caravan had settled into the formation it would take for the rest of the journey. People were creatures of habit. If Hamid the Persian, dealer in silks, wools and other fine fabrics, took his place in line between Meesang the Sayam, buyer and seller of precious and semi-precious gemstones, and Wasim the Pashtun, purveyor of copper goods, one morning, chances were he could be found traveling between these two worthies for the duration of the trip.

Johanna reveled in the freedom of the Road with every league gained in distance from Cambaluc. On the Road it didn't matter that her eyes were too round or that she was too tall or that her hair was the wrong color. There was no enforced separation of races on the Road, on the Road she didn't have to be careful not to speak the Mongol tongue within the hearing of Mongol ears. Persian, Jew, Turgesh, Sogdian, Persian, Frank, Chinese, it did not matter. They were all one to Uncle Cheng, and for the duration of the trip his was the only authority to which they bowed. It was all the stronger because they had surrendered to it voluntarily, for the safety of one meant the safety of all.

In the meantime, she, Jaufre and Shasha were meeting old friends. One such they encountered at their first camp. "Johanna! Johanna!"

Johanna looked toward the sound of her voice. "Fatima!" she said.

The slim, dark girl ran up to her and embraced her with enthusiasm, laughing with pleasure. Fatima, daughter of Ahmed the baker and Malala his wife, was in fact a child of laughter, a pretty girl of Johanna's age, wearing a short jacket over a tunic and an ankle-length skirt, all heavy with colorful embroidery, with unbound hair confined beneath a spangled blue veil. "But what is this! What are you doing on the Road this early? Usually I don't see you until Kashgar." She looked around. "But where is Wu Li?"

She was put in possession of recent events and her laughter faded, but only momentarily, and indeed Johanna could not wish otherwise. "And Shasha," Fatima said, leaving Johanna to embrace the other woman. "And Jaufre," she said, turning to him. Fatima was also something of a flirt. She ran an appraising eye over his long length. "Much...taller," she said. "Than when I last saw you."

She hugged him, too, for what seemed like a much longer time than she had Johanna or Shasha.

Jaufre grinned down at her. "Why, thank you, Fatima. And how is Azar these days?"

Fatima released him, laughing. "Azar is just fine, Jaufre the Frank, and thank you for asking."

"Are you married yet?"

Fatima looked at Jaufre with a speculative eye. "Not yet. I'm waiting to see if I get a better offer."

Jaufre laughed at this. Johanna frowned. Shasha noticed.

"We are joining your caravan, did you know?" Fatima said. "We let our last leave without us because Father said the caravan master didn't know where he was going."

There was general rejoicing, and plans were made immediately to pitch their camps together. Shasha didn't think that either Johanna or Jaufre noticed how ably Johanna was able to keep herself between Jaufre and Fatima at all times.

They made new friends, too, as the journey continued. One of the most interesting was Félicien the Frank, a thin young man with curious eyes in a sun-burned face and dark, untidy curls confined by a floppy cap. His bare cheek proclaimed his youth and his worn but sturdy clothes a purse only irregularly full. His only possessions were a lute and an aged donkey whose complaints in transit could be heard from one end of the caravan to the other. Félicien was not a trader, but a traveler, he told them one evening around the communal campfire. "A goliard, they call us sometimes where I come from," he said.

"Where do you come from?" Johanna said.

"What's a goliard?" Jaufre said.

"A goliard is a student," Félicien said.

"A student," Jaufre said. "Of what?"

Félicien waved an airy hand. "Oh, of the world, my dear Jaufre. Of the world and all its manifest glories."

"How long have you been, ah, studying the world?"

"This will be my third summer on the Road."

"So long," Johanna said, who had noticed that Félicien had not answered her question about where he was from. "How do you pay your way? If you don't trade..." The goliard was lean but not thin, so he wasn't starving.

Félicien quirked an eyebrow, but it appeared he recognized the genuine curiosity behind a question posed by a life made possible and prosperous by trade. "I tell stories," he said. "I sing. I write cansos, and, if I'm paid well enough to hire a fast horse afterward, I write sirventes."

"You sing?" Johanna said.

"What's a canso?" Jaufre said.

"What stories?" Shasha said.

Félicien laughed, displaying a set of very fine teeth, even and white and well cared-for, an unusual sight in a Frank. "Yes, I sing. A canso is a love song. What stories—oh, all stories, any story that will find a few coins in my pocket afterward. But King Arthur and the Round Table a speciality." He gave a slight bow.

"What's a sirvente?" Jaufre said, stumbling a little over the word.

Félicien grimaced. "A hate song," he said, and would be drawn no farther into the subject. Instead he sang them a lilting ditty in the Frankish tongue that he translated into Persian on the fly, about an unlovely swineherd and a passing poet that had everyone around the fire rocking with laughter. Johanna understood much more than she would have before Edyk and the three days at the summerhouse, and laughed along with the rest.

Félicien's voice was high and clear and pure and he could put a soulful quaver into the most mundane verse, causing gentlemen to clear their throats and ladies to wipe surreptitiously at the corners of their eyes. He ended his impromptu concert with a short song called "A Monk's View."

*O wandering clerks*
*You go to Chartres*
*To learn the arts*
*O wandering clerks*
*By the Tyrrhenian*
*You study Aesclepion*
*O wandering clerks*
*Toledo teaches*
*Alchemy and sleight-of-hand*

*O wandering clerks*
*You learn the arts*
*Medicine and magic*
*O wandering clerks*
*Nowhere learn*
*Manners or morals*
*O wandering clerks*

It scanned and rhymed in French, and by then everyone was shouting along whenever the line "O wandering clerks!" made an appearance. At the finish Félicien leapt to his feet and flourished his cap in an elaborate bow. Quite a few coins were tossed into it. Laughter in this case was demonstrably more than its own reward. Johanna took thoughtful note.

From that evening forward Félicien found himself at their campfire more often than not. His stories were in high demand and his voice a welcome addition to their own. He was also a font of information on places beyond the Middle Sea, and Jaufre drank all these in thirstily, especially any scrap concerning Britannia.

Their course took them not directly west; rather, they moved from city to city as trading opportunities and market values offered opportunity. The topography was initially mostly flat, dry plain, sandy dunes interspersed with expanses of loose black pebbles and hard-packed dirt. The Tian Shan Mountains, snow-capped peaks keeping august distance from the riffraff, were succeeded by the Flaming Mountains, which formed a bare rock wall against the northwestern horizon. "They aren't flaming," Johanna said, disappointed that they didn't live up to their name.

"They aren't really of a height to deserve the term 'mountains,' either," Jaufre said critically.

The barely undulating plain was interrupted just often enough for comfortable travel by oasis towns, built on rivers that snaked back and forth for a few leagues before vanishing into the ground, only to reappear again leagues away. The ruins of ancient villages perched on yellow sandstone wedges, marooned high in the air by the erosion of the water's flow. Tiny farms were tucked in along the riverbanks, fields of cotton beginning to bud between straight rows of slender poplars radiant in silvery green. Grape vines sent investigatory tendrils across wooden frames and fruit trees were small white clouds of blooms. Everywhere the bees were happily drunk on nectar, buzzing dizzyingly from blossom to blossom.

In Lanchow they traded not at all, the city being too near Chang'an and Cambaluc for profit such as Wu Li had taught them to expect. If they did not trade, however, they could look to see what luxuries were going for the highest prices that year, and store that information away for future profit. Midway between the spice market and a row of apothecaries shops Johanna, Jaufre and Félicien were offered a full saddlebag of grayish grainy matter that the seller, hand on his heart, earnestly swore upon the bones of his ancestors was dried ground testicle of Jacob's sheep, a proven aphrodisiac— "Guaranteed to warm the coldest woman on the darkest winter night, sahib!" The seller, a wizened little man in a filthy jellaba and an even filthier turban fastened with a chipped red brooch that couldn't even pretend to be a ruby, clutched at Jaufre's sleeve. "Yes, yes, and a known curative for shingles, croup, headache, stomach ache and toothache besides!" When Jaufre smiled and shook his head the old man said, "Where else will you find such rare and wonderful goods, young sir? Where?"

"Where, indeed," Johanna said, but Jaufre was made of kinder stuff and pressed a small coin into the old man's hand. It disappeared, but they left the old man pulling his wispy beard and calling out after them, "Is it Wuwei that you journey to next? No, no, not Wuwei, young sir, young miss, as your life depends upon it! Those fellows on the other side of the river are robbers and murderers, they are deviants and pederasts, they rape their mothers, they slay their fathers! Stay safe here where you deal always with honest men! I spit, I spit—" suiting his word to the deed so that Jaufre had to step quickly out of range "—all good people spit on the monsters there!"

"Well, we can't say we haven't been warned," Félicien said, and Johanna could tell by the faraway look in his eyes that he was already composing his next song, something scurrilous to do with the perverse occupations of the dread Wuwei-ers, no doubt.

They met Shasha coming out of the spice market. "Anything worth buying?" Jaufre said.

"I will wait for Yarkent," Shasha said, and Jaufre and Johanna laughed. Félicien looked between them, quizzical, and Johanna said, "Just wait. When we get to Yarkent, you'll see."

In Wuwei, the Lanchow marketplace prophet's dire prophecies notwithstanding, Johanna found a Khuree merchant with two bales of sable pelts, so expertly cured they rivaled silk for suppleness and sheen. The Khuree knew what he had and the bargaining was fierce, but in the end Johanna bore the sables off in triumph, secure in the knowledge that the return on investment to be had farther down the Road would be well worth her while.

Jaufre found a smith who made belt knives of simple yet elegant design, with edges honed to a sharpness that, the smith said with pride, "cut your eye just to look at it." Jaufre tested a few of the edges and the smith wasn't far wrong. They were beautiful and useful and small in bulk and weight, a hundred of them tucked easily into a single pack.

Shasha visited the spice bazaar and said, "I will wait for Yarkent."

"What's in Yarkent?" Félicien said again, and again Jaufre and Johanna would only shake their heads.

In Kuche the donkey carts were tethered in the dry riverbed as the muezzin's call to prayer summoned their drivers to the mosque. On Saturday the sun rose on a bustling market. Jaufre found a vendor with two camel load's worth of fragrant sandalwood that he knew would do well in Kashgar. Johanna sought out a wool merchant with whom Wu Li had a long and profitable relationship, who could be relied upon not to leave his bales open in transit so as to gather desert sand on the road and so increase their weight, although she kneaded a handful before making an offer because it was expected of her father's daughter. The wool merchant offered her hot, sweet mint tea and commiseration upon the loss of such a noble father, and she bought ten bales of his finest wool for a weaver in Kashgar who would know how to value it.

Shasha, upon inquiry, said with a certain self-conscious dignity that she had seen nothing of interest beyond an inferior frankincense priced so high as to be amusing to any experienced trader.

"And you'll wait for Yarkent," Jaufre said.

Johanna laughed, and Shasha glared, and the three of them returned to camp in high spirits.

"Honorable niece," Uncle Cheng said, intercepting them before their yurt.

"Honorable uncle," Johanna said, wondering at the twinkle in his eye. "Have you prospered in Kuche?"

"I have," he said, the twinkle more pronounced. "I believe I may prosper even more tomorrow."

"We remain another night then, uncle?" Jaufre said.

"We do," Uncle Cheng said with a slight bow and a beaming smile that made all three of them instantly suspicious. "We do indeed."

"Is the market extended for another day?"

"It is not," Uncle Cheng said. "But there are to be races."

Jaufre and Shasha both watched with foreboding as Johanna's expression changed to resemble Uncle Cheng's in a way no two persons who looked so infinitely dissimilar should do.

Race day dawned in Kuche clear and cool, the aromas of baking bread and animal manure jostling for place. Jaufre woke to find Johanna already gone, and looked across the yurt to see Shasha staring back at him. "This is not wise," she said. "It will draw attention."

"What," he said, grumbling his way into his clothes, "you think Edyk the Portuguese hasn't noticed yet that his horse is missing?"

The dry riverbed had been transformed, all the donkey carts moved to the sides and tethered to roots beneath the overhang. The center of the riverbed was taken up with a group of child acrobats who tumbled down gracefully from quickly-formed human pyramids to somersault between running camels. A strongman, an ex-soldier by the contemptuous curl of his lip, bent a sword in half, then straightened it out again. A magician made a little girl's doll disappear, made it reappear when the little girl opened her mouth to cry, and then produced a silver drachma from her brother's ear. Lines formed before letter writers, spare quills tucked behind their ears, their assistants scraping industriously at previous letters written on already venerable pieces of vellum. An astrologer was doing a rousing business in horoscopes, musicians piped their pipes and strummed their sitars and beat their drums with greater and lesser skill, and the inevitable Kuchean dancing girls entranced wide-eyed country boys with hips that seemed to move independently of the rest of their bodies. Or they did before the boys' mothers came up to smack their ears and chase them back to their families, there to fall victim to the prostitutes beckoning seductively from the trees growing along the top of the riverbank.

There were at last five men taking bets, by Jaufre's count. The first race was a donkey race, their riders children waving colorful banners. At least half the children fell off at the start, one let his banner become tangled in his donkey's hooves and the donkey fell and his rider with him, and the winner crossed the finish line going backwards. Most of the bettors were parents, and two over-excited fathers fell into an argument that deteriorated into fisticuffs and had to be separated before the next race, to the vociferous dismay of the bystanders who had been placing bets on the outcome.

The second race was between camels, long, lean racing beasts with light racing saddles and professional riders, small, wiry men who listened to their owners' last-minute advice with impassive expressions before throwing a leg over their mounts and kicking them groaning and spitting to their feet. Ten of them lined up for the start and all ten disappeared around the first bend in the river, their progress reported on by shouting, red-faced men stationed above. Betting would continue until the halfway mark, when one of the men waved a black flag violently back and forth and the touts stepped down from their rocks. A few minutes later a roar began far off and increased as the racers drew nearer.

The camels burst round the last bend in the river, brown blurs with their noses stretched out in front of them and ungainly legs kicking sand up all the way back to Cambaluc. They had been slow off the mark but they more than made up for it now, and Jaufre found himself yelling along with everyone else as the two leading camels flashed across the finish line.

There was some considerable conversation between the racers, the owners and the spectators as to who had won. In the end it came down to an older gentleman of dignified mien and snow-white turban, who tucked his hands in his cuffs and delivered his verdict. Half the crowd groaned and the other half cheered and lined up for their winnings. The touts looked relieved, so the favorite must have won. Jaufre couldn't tell one camel from another and he hadn't placed any bets so the matter was less pressing to him.

The sun was overhead and the scene devolved into a talking, laughing, jostling crowd reliving the camel race second by second. The acrobats came back out, and the Kuche dance troupe, and men and women appeared bearing trays of pomegranate juice and rounds of bread and dried apricots and almonds roasted with salt. A puppet show told the story of a Mongol soldier who eloped with the sultan's daughter, who then died of the smell of her affianced on the first night, eliciting gales of laughter and a respectable handful of coins. A tightrope walker stretched a rope between two trees and held a crowd of people breathless as he jumped, skipped, leaped and did handsprings twenty feet above the river bed. A very talented contortionist made everyone uncomfortable and three jugglers tossed flaming torches back and forth as if they were apples. The torches disappeared and were replaced by knives, which disappeared in their turn to be replaced by duck eggs. Each of the jugglers caught an egg in each hand and one in their mouths without breaking any, and bowed to much applause.

This seemed to be the signal to clear the course for the next race, and there was no mistaking the air of excitement that rippled over the crowd.

"A great event in these parts, evidently."

Jaufre turned to see Sheik Mohammed standing next to him. Immaculate as ever in white robes, his jeweled knife tucked into his belt, his son Farhad standing next to him and the two omnipresent guards alert behind. He surveyed the crowd along the river bed with an aloof expression. He didn't quite draw his skirts in so as not to be polluted by contact with common folk, but nevertheless managed to give the distinct impression that he was entitled to reascend to his own social level at any given moment, and would do so upon the least provocation.

"There is almost always a race in Kuche," Jaufre said.

"So it seems. Do you have a horse in the race?"

"I don't," Jaufre said, and if the sheik noticed the emphasis Jaufre placed on the first word he took no notice. "Do you?"

"I do," the sheik said. He grinned, and it was a surprisingly friendly grin, albeit with an edge to it. "And you would be advised to bet on it, Jaufre of Cambaluc."

Jaufre felt a smile spread across his face. "Would I?" he said.

Soon afterward the contestants lined up, and Jaufre felt the sheik stiffen next to him. He turned his face away so that the sheik couldn't see his grin.

North Wind was the only all-white horse among the racers, and Johanna the only female rider. There was some murmuring about this in the crowd, but Kuche was a caravan town and had seen many more odd things in its day. Then someone recognized her. "Wu Li's daughter! Wu Li's daughter! Wu Li's daughter!" Her name was shouted in Persian and Mandarin, in Uigur and Mongol, in Armenian and what Jaufre thought might have been Hebrew, but it was a long time since he'd heard it. No matter. They remembered Johanna, and Wu Li, in Kuche.

Johanna laughed out loud and waved first to one side of the crowd and then the other. It was only the most curmudgeonly of watchers who did not recognize the joy and pride she took in her horse.

Not that he was hers, Jaufre thought, and scanned the crowd for an officer of the court, merely out of habit.

"A bet on the Honorable Wu Li's daughter and her fine steed, young sir?"

Jaufre looked down to meet the bland eyes of Shasha, stick of charcoal poised over a rough wood tablet, her leather purse heavy at her waist, Félicien guarding her back, and stifled a laugh. Shasha gave an imperceptible shrug, as if to say, What else was I supposed to do?

"No?" she said. "And you, fine sir? A late entrant, to be sure, and untested this far west, but surely worthy of the wager?"

The sheik gave Shasha a sharp glance. "If I bet, I bet on my own horse, madam."

Shasha bent her head. "My apologies, fine sir," she said, and vanished discreetly into the crowd, Félicien a step behind her. A few moments later Jaufre heard her voice. "A bet on the white horse? Of course, my fine sirs, of course! The odds? Come, come, you have only to look at him! The sheik's horse is known never to have a lost a race? Then it is time he did, and I say the white stallion is the one to do it! Ten to one? Eight to one? Very well, five to one, and welcome, fine sir!"

Jaufre very carefully did not look at the man next to him, but on the sheik's other side his son choked and turned it quickly into a cough when his father glared at him.

The sheik's horse was easy to spot, an Arab stallion with a gleaming mahogany coat clothing a fine collection of muscle and bone. He danced impatiently on small, neat hooves, ready to be off. His rider kept glancing at Johanna as if he couldn't believe his eyes. Jaufre felt the sheik shift and still himself again with a palpable effort. Looking that impervious all the time must come with a price.

"How can you bear it?" the sheik's son said to Jaufre in an undertone.

"Bear what?" Jaufre said, his eyes like the sheik's son's trained on the woman on the white stallion.

"Your woman's face uncovered before so many men's eyes," Farhad, the sheik's son, said.

"She's not my woman," Jaufre said. Not yet, he thought.

He didn't notice the sheik's son coming to attention next to him at his words.

The race official cried out and the crowd fell silent, all eyes on the starting line and the seven horses standing there in relative degrees of serenity. The sheik's stallion looked ready to explode out of its skin, North Wind looked carved from marble, and the other five horses simply faded out of existence by comparison. Voices went up as last frantic bids were made. Jaufre didn't see Uncle Cheng but he was sure he was in the crowd somewhere with silver coin running through his fingers like water.

The official, perched above the fray on the edge of the river's bank, counted to three. At two the sheik's mahogany stallion quivered all over and strained at the bit. North Wind looked bored. The official cried out "Go!" His arm dropped sharply.

And North Wind went from a period of calm repose, probably speculating on the content of his next meal, to a full-length extended gallop in one stride.

Jaufre had seen it before, many times, and it never failed to amaze him. Johanna lay flat on North Wind's back, her face pressed against his neck, her hands buried in his mane. She rode him bareback—"North Wind would never allow me to fall"—with her knees drawn up and her heels pressed tightly against his sides. Her braid was blown free in three strides, on the fourth they were passing Jaufre's position and on the seventh they had reached the first bend.

"Allah forfend!" the sheik said. "What a horse!"

But Jaufre had eyes only for Johanna. So did the sheik's son, although Jaufre didn't notice.

The ground shook beneath the thud of hooves striking sand and North Wind was a full length ahead of the sheik's stallion as they went out of sight, and five lengths ahead of him when they thundered back across the finish line ten minutes later. Here, North Wind deigned to prance and preen, just a bit. The stallion snapped at him and North Wind moved neatly out of reach and nipped the stallion's rider on the thigh, startling something very like a squeal out of him.

And quite right, too, Jaufre thought, shoving his way through the crowd. "Congratulations," he said to Johanna, who brought her leg over North Wind's neck and slid neatly to the ground.

She shook her head, hands busily reassembling her braid. "It wasn't fair, really. No other horse here had a chance against North Wind."

The rider of the mahogany stallion overheard her and reddened.

"No," another voice said. "They didn't."

The stallion's rider paled, and Jaufre turned to see that Sheik Mohammed had followed him through the crowd. The sheik's son was next to him and this time Jaufre saw him look at Johanna, his admiration evident.

"Surely he is a descendant of Bucephalus himself," the sheik said to Jaufre. "I will buy him from you."

"He's not mine," Jaufre said shortly.

The sheik gave him an incredulous look, and turned to Johanna.

He's not hers, either, Jaufre thought.

"I will buy your horse, then," the sheik said to Johanna, reluctantly and somewhat uncomfortably, as if he was unaccustomed to speaking directly to women.

"Certainly," Johanna said with a glittering smile.

"Name your price," the sheik said.

North Wind poked his nose over Johanna's shoulder and blew in her ear. "All the gold in Byzantium, all the pearls in Cipangu, and all the rubies in Mien," she said, with a grin at Jaufre, and at Shasha and Félicien as they arrived, out of breath. Shasha was carrying a noticeably heavier purse. "There is no price too high for North Wind. Besides, I can't sell him."

The sheik reached out a hand and North Wind's teeth snapped again, short of their target only because Johanna said in firm voice, "No." She patted his neck. "I would be cheating you, sheik. He wouldn't go with you if I did sell him. There is no rope strong enough to tie him to you while I am still in the world. He would savage every other horse and trample every guard and break down every door in your stables, to make his way back to me. He's done it before. And he would certainly never allow your man on his back."

"That," Jaufre said reluctantly, "is really true." He reflected on Edyk's troubles with riders, or more specifically on North Wind's troubles with riders. Any races he had run were won in spite of them, and Edyk had forfeited more than one race because North Wind had dumped his rider before the finish line. No rider had ever volunteered for a second race on North Wind's broad back.

Jaufre looked at Johanna in sudden realization. She met his eyes, a smile in her own.

"He followed you down from the summerhouse," Jaufre said later.

She nodded. "I tried to leave him in his stall at Edyk's, but he kicked it down and came after me. I think, somehow, he knew, and he would not be left behind."

She was grooming North Wind, who had been fed and watered and who was now picketed and drowsing with his weight on three legs. He was almost purring beneath the rhythmic stroke of the bristles.

"And I didn't want to miss the ceremony for Father," Johanna said, "and by then it was too late."

"Why didn't you tell us?"

"If you could have seen your expressions when I rode up! I couldn't resist, Jaufre."

Her grin was impish, her eyes twinkling, her voice on the edge of laughter. He knew no other woman who would be so unconcerned that he had thought her guilty of such an enormous theft. His hand went out but she had turned back to North Wind and didn't see it.

She smoothed out a nonexistent tangle and stepped back, North Wind gleaming in the evening light. They were staying another night in Kuche on the strength of Wu Cheng's winnings. Uncle Cheng even now was hosting an uproarious party for the city's dignitaries behind city walls, catered by every food vendor and wine merchant within a day's ride. It would very likely continue until they were ready to depart the following evening.

"Sheik Mohammed is serious about buying him," Jaufre said.

"North Wind is just as serious about not being bought," Johanna said, and took her leave of her equine familiar with a last, loving stroke. "There are new baths in the city," she said. "Shasha went ahead. Shall we?"

# · Twelve ·

*Kuche*

———

The water was hot and the attendants scrubbed hard. As they emerged again into the street an hour later, not far away they could hear the sounds of people still enjoying their wine at Uncle Cheng's expense. "Should we join them?" Jaufre said.

Johanna yawned hugely. "I'm for bed." She smiled at him, her face still flushed from her bath.

Without knowing he did it, Jaufre raised a hand and brushed back a wayward bronze curl that had escaped from her damp braid to tangle in her eyelashes.

Johanna's smile faded and they stood staring at each other.

Shasha cleared her throat. "Bed, yes, indeed," she said. "It's been a long day."

They both jumped. Jaufre shook his head as if trying to clear it and without a word turned on his heel.

Johanna stood where she was, her mouth half open, watching Jaufre's receding back.

She had not thought of love beyond Edyk. If things had been different she might have married him and lived with him and borne his children and traveled and traded with him. Leaving him had been the most difficult thing she had ever done.

The Road had taught her that no one, man or woman, was ever quite done with love, but she had never applied that knowledge to her own life. Perhaps it was simply because she hadn't had time, she thought now.

After all, they were not even five hundred leagues from Cambaluc. It was only a little over a month since the idyll in the lake house. She could still feel Edyk's lips against hers, her body rising to his, the joy they had taken in each other's response. It wasn't as if she didn't ache for him, as if the hunger she had felt then had stopped the instant she passed beneath the Great West Gate of Cambaluc. She had dreamed of his hands on her, only to wake, heart pounding, restless, wanting, reaching for him.

She had no doubt that she could find physical relief with any one of the men she saw looking at her in that way. But if the Road had taught her much truth about the relations between men and women, her parents had showed her that such relations could be very good and very lasting. She was well aware that most marriages were transactional, trading a child for a stake in a business, or a foothold in an influential family, or simply a dowry big enough to provide for both children and their children for life.

Or as a convenient way to dispose of an unwanted stepdaughter.

Jaufre had always been there beside her, her fellow trader, her brother in arms, her co-conspirator in whatever devilry their fertile minds could devise. She had felt Jaufre's hands on her a thousand, a thousand thousand times over the years, throwing her up into the saddle, steadying her hands on a new bow, nudging her elbow to the proper position in Fair Lady Works at Shuttles before Deshi the Scout saw that she was wildly out of form. There was no one with whom she felt more comfortable than Jaufre.

This, though. The way his eyes seemed to darken as he watched his hand slide the lock of hair back behind her ear. The touch of his fingers on the skin of her cheek, a touch that seemed to sear straight down through her body, igniting feelings that she had only ever felt for Edyk. She looked down, bewildered, to see her nipples hard against the silk of her tunic, and the dark hollow between her legs felt as if it were about to open, hot, slippery, welcoming.

"Coming?" Shasha said blandly, and like Jaufre, bereft of words, Johanna followed her.

The caravansary in Kuche was undergoing restoration ("The Kuche caravansary has been under construction since before I was born," Johanna had said upon hearing the news) and Uncle Cheng had set up camp outside the walls, arranging their goods and sleeping tents at the heart of a circle of livestock in turn inside a circle of constantly patrolling guards. Their yurt was next to Uncle Cheng's, and the pickets for their mounts on the other side of the guards' tents. It was the safest possible place in the caravan. Even the most accomplished thief would not have dreamed of trying his luck there.

Which was why, perhaps among other reasons, they were taken completely by surprise. Johanna saw Jaufre duck under the flap and heard him stumble and swear.

"What's wrong, Jaufre?" Shasha said, following him inside. Johanna caught the flap before it closed. It dropped behind her and the light from the torches that lit the camp only dimly in the first place was cut off.

The yurt seemed to explode. Something hit her in the chest and she staggered back into the wall of the canvas, which sagged precariously beneath her weight. "What—" Some disturbance of the air warned her at the last minute and she let herself slip to the ground as something large passed over her head. There was a loud metallic clang and an oath from Jaufre, followed by the sound of flesh striking flesh. They were under attack, she thought, incredulous.

The fight was all the more eerie because it was so quiet. Johanna heard Jaufre grunt with effort, she heard Shasha panting, although she could barely hear either over the heart trying to jump out of her chest. She decided to change that and scrambled to her feet, shouting at the top of her voice. "Help! Help! Thieves! Help! Help! Thieves in the camp, help, help, help!"

Outside the tent she heard a distant whinny. Inside the tent there was a guttural curse in a voice that sounded familiar but to which she could not put a name, and then a thud. Another smack of flesh on flesh, and Shasha cried out.

"Shasha!" Johanna said. "Help, thieves, help, thieves!" She fumbled in the dark for the tent flap but it was too dark and she was all turned around.

There was a sound of swiftly approaching thunder, which confused her. It was a cloudless night with a sky full of stars. There could be no approaching storm, and then there was one, in the shape of eleven hundredweight of furious horse, who charged into the yurt at full speed and laid about him indiscriminately with hoof and teeth.

"North Wind!"

"Ouch!"

"Johanna, get outside and calm that beast down!"

Two slashing hooves brought the yurt down around them, tent poles cracking, ropes loosening into an inextricable tangle, and Johanna caught a sliver of light and dove through the opening seconds before she would have been caught in the mess. Above her, North Wind, magnificent in his rage, bugled a war cry through his nose and prepared to renew his assault. She darted in to grasp his halter and before he could rear again let all of her weight dangle from it.

He threw up his head and whinnied, still lunging and rearing and dropping his hooves with a fine lack of discrimination for private property, in his fury bringing down the yurt next to theirs. Fatima and Malala and Ahmed were going to be very annoyed. Fortunately no cries of distress were heard from inside. Like everyone else they must still be in the city and in the very short space of time granted her for coherent thought she was deeply grateful.

She released the halter to throw her arms around his neck and wiggled her way onto his back, laying flat, arms and legs tight around him. "It's all right, boy, it's all right, now, calm down, calm down, it's me, I'm all right." She kept talking, nonsense words mostly, hoping the sound of her voice would calm him. Even then he nearly had her off twice, and when he finally recognized that it was indeed Johanna on his back he reached back with his head, snatched a mouthful of tunic and hauled her down to the ground, where he proceeded to examine her stem to stern with his nose.

"Stop it! North Wind! Stop it! Let me up! I'm fine! By all the Mongol gods, I'm fine!"

From the corner of her eye she saw a figure struggle free of the collapsed yurt and race off, but it was too dark to see who it was. A second figure followed the first and this time North Wind helped him on his way with a judicious kick from his right hind leg. It caught the fleeing man squarely in the seat of the pants and raised him a good two ells in the air. Confounding all expectation he landed on his feet, staggered a few steps and was unfortunately at speed by the time Jaufre had fought himself free of the wreck, vanishing into the thicket of yurts surrounding them.

Jaufre rooted around in the debris to extricate Shasha. North Wind grudgingly allowed Johanna back on her feet. By this time many people had responded to Johanna's shouts and North Wind's battle cry, including Félicien, who stared wide-eyed at the wreckage of the yurt and at the scrapes and bruises sustained by his friends, none of whom by great good fortune were worse hurt. Many of the others had only just returned home from drinking a great deal at Uncle Cheng's expense and were much more jolly than the occasion warranted. They weren't much help getting the yurt back up, either.

"I knew racing North Wind was a bad idea," Shasha said.

She was sporting a spectacular pair of black eyes. Jaufre had a cut on his cheek extending from his right temple almost to the corner of his mouth. It was very thin, as if made by an extraordinarily sharp blade. All three of them were bruised and stiff.

Johanna held up her mother's Robe of a Thousand Larks. It had been slashed nearly in two, the collar alone holding the garment together. The embroidered birds on the cut edge were already beginning to unravel. "Why didn't they just steal it?" she said, fighting tears.

Shasha, tight-lipped, looked up. "They didn't even bother to unbuckle my pack, they just cut it open."

Jaufre held up his own pack, now in two pieces, in reply.

The smells of cumin and cinnamon and coriander permeated the yurt and Jaufre tied back the flap to air it out. He felt the comforting weight of his father's sword resting along his spine and was grateful that his most prized possession was never out of his sight. He found himself leaning over to finger the reassuring lumps in the hem of his coat, and looked up to see Shasha doing the same.

"They took nothing," he said, frowning at the pile he had made of his belongings.

"Or they didn't find what they were looking for," Shasha said.

Johanna said nothing.

Uncle Cheng, red of eye and short of temper, summoned his havildar. This was Firas, a wiry man of middle height with a sparse beard and a scimitar with a grip bound in leather so frequently in use it looked as if it had been molded to fit his and only his hand. He was new to them and indeed to Uncle Cheng, having held the post of head of guard for less than two years. He followed them back to the yurt once it was light enough to see, and surveyed the scene with dark, remote eyes. "Did you see anyone?"

He spoke to Jaufre in Farsi and Johanna answered in kind. "We were at the baths. When we came back, they were inside the yurt, and attacked us as we entered."

"Nothing at all?" he said, again to Jaufre. "No strangers loitering around?"

"You heard her," Shasha said. "Do you think we would have left the tent unguarded, that we wouldn't have sounded the alarm if we had suspected something like this might happen?"

He looked at her for a long moment, and then bent his head in a gesture somewhere between a nod and a bow. "As you say. Do you have any idea yet what is missing?"

"That's just it," Jaufre said. "Nothing seems to be missing. Cut open, ripped apart, but not missing."

Firas meditated for a moment, his eyes dwelling for a moment on Jaufre's sword. "A fortunate circumstance. Or happy forethought."

"Perhaps both," Shasha said. "Old No—the honorable Wu Cheng's hospitality was offered to all in the camp and in the city. The camp was nearly deserted when we came back from the baths. What self-respecting thief would pass up such an opportunity?"

"There were guards," Firas said mildly.

"Not that anyone would notice," Shasha said with acid precision.

His eyes returned to her and she thought he almost smiled. "As you say," he said again. "Still, one must consider all the possibilities. Have you recently turned off any servants who might be nursing a grudge? Dealt with a merchant who might think you had cheated him? Offended an ex-lover?"

"None of those things," Johanna said, and then looked at Jaufre.

"What?" he said.

"That fat redheaded dancer in Dunhuang," she said.

He reddened. "That short Portuguese trader in Cambaluc," he said.

In the subsequent smoldering silence, Shasha cleared her throat delicately. "No," she said, "nothing like that, havildar. At least not recently."

Their eyes met in understanding. "I will inquire," he said, and this time it was a genuine bow, denoting respect and admiration for one newly met.

Shasha waited until he was gone. "All right, Johanna."

Johanna looked at her, surprised at the sharp edge to the other woman's voice. "What?" she said.

"What's in your purse?" Shasha said.

"What?" Jaufre said.

Johanna blushed a fiery red to the roots of her hair. "I don't know what you're talking about."

"Oh yes, you do," Shasha said. "You've been riding with your chin on your shoulder since we left Cambaluc. He—" she jerked her head at Jaufre "—thinks it's because you're pining for Edyk. I think it's because you think we might be pursued." She gestured at the mess in the yurt. "And now I think that we have been, and that they've caught up to us."

"I don't know what you're talking about," Johanna said, but her hand went to the leather purse at her waist.

"What?" Jaufre said again.

"Whatever you took, it put us in danger." Shasha snatched the Robe of a Thousand Larks from Johanna's hands. "You could have been wearing this when it was sliced into pieces."

Johanna flinched and Shasha tossed the robe aside. "I love you, Johanna, I'd lay down my life for yours and so would Jaufre, but we have a right to know why."

Jaufre didn't say "What?" a third time because it might sound like it was the only word he knew.

They waited.

"Oh, all right," Johanna said, sighing. She fumbled at her waist and opened the purse, holding it out to display what was inside.

Jaufre blinked and opened his mouth, but was able to produce only a splutter.

Shasha put her hand over her eyes and shook her head. "Johanna. Johanna. What were you thinking, girl?"

"Pursued?" Jaufre said, finding his vocabulary and gaining in volume. "There is at minimum a band of hired mercenaries on our trail, if not an entire imperial cohort!"

Nestled inside the leather purse was the jade box containing the Wu bao.

Tucked in cozily next to it was Wu Li's worn, leather-bound journal.

Baos were hereditary, increasing in value as they aged from generation to generation. New ones were awarded only rarely and usually only after a lifetime spent proving one's worth as a trader, or after an especially hefty bribe. Penalties for forgeries were harsh, which only began with stripping the offender of the right to trade in Everything Under the Heavens, and usually ending in prison. In short, the widow Wu would be unable to conduct the business of the Wu Li trading consortium without the Wu Li bao, and certainly, Jaufre thought bitterly, a mercenary troop's fee would be less expensive than the extortionate bribery necessary to moving a petition for a new bao through the bureaucracy at court.

As for the journal...In a faint voice Shasha said, "The journal? You took Wu Li's journal, too?"

"They were my father's," Johanna said. "And now they are mine."

"You do realize that the Honorable Wu Li's second wife may disagree?" Jaufre said with awful sarcasm.

"Of course she does," Shasha said. The strength in her legs gave out, as much from Johanna's revelation as from the lumps she had taken in the recent fracas, and she sat down with a thump on the nearest tangle of belongings. "She knows perfectly well that Wu Li's widow is sure to be nothing short of enraged. That's why she stole them." She raised her head. "Isn't it, Johanna?"

"Well, she certainly didn't see fit to give them to me as part of my dowry," Johanna said. "As she most certainly should have done."

Shasha cast her eyes heavenward for guidance.

"Johanna," Jaufre said in a controlled voice, "you understand, don't you, that without the bao, Dai Fang will be unable to trade commercially? At least until she's able to get a new one?"

"And that that could take years?" Shasha said.

"And that even if she does manage to acquire her own bao that her tithe will increase? Which will cut significantly into her profits?"

"And that even if she can get a new one quicker than that, that you hold the keys to the entire Li network in Wu Li's journal?" Shasha said. "That she won't know the names of debtors or agents in Kashgar or Antioch or Alexandria, or the names of Wu trading partners anywhere along the Road?"

Johanna grinned. "No, she won't, will she?" The other two were rendered momentarily speechless, and Johanna seized her advantage. "You're not worried that she'll follow us, are you? The Dishonorable Dai Fang wouldn't dream of subjecting herself to the barbarian practices of any race so unfortunate as to find itself living outside the borders of Everything Under the Heavens."

"Oh, agreed," Jaufre said.

"Of course she wouldn't," Shasha said.

"But Gokudo would," Jaufre said.

A thoughtful silence fell.

"If she ordered him to, Johanna," Jaufre said, "he would carve all three of us into bite-size pieces with that pig-sticker of his." And he would enjoy it, he thought. He raised his hand to the wound on his cheek. Gokudo had displayed the sharpness of the blade on his naginata many times. If indeed one of last night's visitors was Gokudo, then they were all very lucky that the samurai had not chosen to attack them in the open.

All three of them looked at the Robe of a Thousand Larks, mutilated with a single, sharp slash, and all of three imagined what would have happened if Johanna had been wearing it when the blade struck.

Johanna was the first to recover. "Nonsense," she said robustly, as if volume and confidence alone could rout what were now, surely, only the ghosts of their past. "If the Dishonorable Dai Fang sent Gokudo after us, she would have sent him at once, the instant she noticed what was missing."

"So?"

"So why did he wait until Kuche to try to get them back?" Johanna said.

"Kuche is the first place we have spent outside caravansary walls," Shasha said.

"Nonsense," Johanna said again, albeit with less certainty. "We made camp in the desert dozens of times."

"Johanna," Jaufre said, with awful patience, "it would be much easier and much safer for Gokudo to hide his presence among the many strangers housed each night in a city, especially a city along the Silk Road. It would be much more difficult to approach an armed, isolated camp the size of ours."

"He's been following us," Shasha said.

"Since Cambaluc," Jaufre said, "waiting his chance."

"And," Johanna said slowly, "Uncle Cheng travels only as far as Kashgar on this trip." She looked at Jaufre, and at Shasha. "After that, we're on our own."

There followed an awkward silence. "I'm not sorry I did it," Johanna said at last. "They were Father's. By right they are now mine." She tucked the bao and book back into her purse and tied it shut. She looked defiant, and righteous, and unrepentant, and a hundred other things that would get them all killed well before Kashgar. "Besides," she said, "we won. They didn't get what they came for, and we ran them off."

Jaufre exchanged a long, expressionless look with Shasha. "As you say," he said at last, echoing the havildar. It was a useful phrase.

"Let's get this mess cleaned up," Shasha said.

Firas, listening on the other side of the canvas wall of the yurt, now slipped silently away.

Later, with Johanna safely out of earshot, Shasha said, "The bao. And the book."

"One or the other I might be able to defend," Jaufre said, trying to work back up to the righteous wrath he had experienced that morning and not quite managing it. "The book, certainly. But both?"

"Not to mention the horse," Shasha said.

He stopped and looked at her. "I completely forgot about the horse." His voice shook. "Do you think Edyk went to the house looking for North Wind?"

Shasha's lips trembled. "Can you imagine what the widow's reaction would have been when she found the bao and the book missing? And then Edyk arriving, demanding the return of North Wind?"

Jaufre started to grin. "I wonder if the Honorable Wu Li's house is still standing."

"Perhaps," she said unsteadily. "Pieces of it." She strove for control. "Still, this is serious, Jaufre."

"Of course you're right," he said. "At the very least we should begin standing watches."

They looked at each other and broke down completely, laughing so immoderately that they had to cling to each other for support. Outside, passersby wondered what was going on in the big yurt that was so funny.

Uncle Cheng delayed their departure for another day while Firas investigated. Meantime, Shasha was summoned to the caravan master's presence and requested to provide something to ease his wine-induced aches and pains. She snorted and brewed him a strong dish of steeped betony, which he gagged over but didn't dare dump out, not under that stern eye. And it did help, he had to admit, later and most reluctantly. At least he stopped feeling as if he were bleeding from his ears.

There were almost two thousand people in their caravan, over five thousand in Kuche and hundreds more in caravans large and small in constant arrival and departure. Everyone within and without the city walls was intent upon the engrossing subjects of their own commerce and trade and profit. There was little interest to be spared for suspicious strangers bent on burglary and mayhem, unless it was burglary and mayhem directed at themselves. Firas' inquiries thus bore little fruit, as he duly reported to Uncle Cheng, to which meeting Uncle Cheng had summoned Jaufre.

"As was to be expected, Uncle Cheng," Jaufre said. "We will keep a stricter guard in future."

He and Firas left together, and Jaufre was about to go his own way when Firas said, "A moment of your time, young sir."

"Havildar?"

"I wonder if I might see your weapon?"

Jaufre hesitated, and then with some reluctance drew his father's sword from its sheath.

Firas examined it with the eye of an expert, holding it up to judge the straightness of the blade, testing the edge, flipping it into the air and catching it again to assess its balance. All of the things, in fact, that Gokudo had done, although Gokudo had done it without permission. The havildar was a weapons master determining the effectiveness of a tool, expert, impartial, interested in an academic way but with no acquisitiveness. Jaufre, watching him, felt himself relax.

"A noble blade, young sir," Firas said, returning it hilt first. "I would see it in practice."

Jaufre felt the blood run up into his face. "It was my father's sword, havildar. He died before he could instruct me."

"Ah." Firas nodded, his eyes resting on something over Jaufre's shoulder. "I myself practice with such of my men who are so inclined at dawn each day before we march. Your blade and ours are of different models, but I would guess that much of the basic moves would be the same."

Jaufre weighed his father's sword. It had always felt somehow right and proper in his hand, a deadly extension of his own muscle and bone. At any time these past five years Jaufre could have asked one of the imperial guards for instruction. He wasn't sure why he had not.

Today, he thought of the items in Johanna's purse, of the fight in the yurt, of Shasha's black eyes and the cut on his cheek. He was good with knife and bow and almost as good as Johanna with the staff. Sword skill he had none. He thought again of the long slash up the back of Shu Ming's Robe of a Thousand Larks, and thought of how Johanna's face looked lit from within whenever she donned it to sing around an evening campfire.

"I am grateful for the invitation, havildar," Jaufre said, sliding sword back into its sheath. "And pleased to accept."

Firas noted how easily the movement was completed. Jaufre's sword was not light in weight. There might be more to this slim young man than met the eye. "Just before dawn then, young sir, beyond the cook tents."

Jaufre was there well before dawn, Johanna at his side, as they worked through the thirty-two movements of soft boxing. They went through them three times, seamless, synchronized, one movement flowing naturally into the next. As the horizon brightened they sank down into horse stance, palms loosely cupped and parallel in front of them, held position for a slow count of ten, and rose smoothly again to a standing position.

"I see, young sir," said a voice behind them, "that while you may not have had lessons in the wielding of your father's sword, you are not entirely deficient in lessons of self defense."

"We were taught the art from a very young age," Johanna said, "by my father's man, Deshi the Scout."

He bowed slightly. "Honor is due such a fine teacher. Is it that I am to instruct the young lady in swordsmanship as well?"

Johanna inclined her head, matching dignity with dignity. "No, havildar, I have no such weapon. Though I would like to observe, if you please." Her voice was mild. Her eyes were not.

Almost, Firas smiled, or so it seemed to Jaufre.

He remembered that first practice for the rest of his life, although there was little of the thrust and parry he would learn later. Light increased in the east, flowing over the horizon onto the broad plain beneath. The hundreds of donkey carts tethered to scrub brush growing from the sandy sides of the river, the churned sand of the river bed the only evidence of yesterday's races. The call of the muezzin. The low curses of men waking, the crackle of cook fires, the smell of bread baking.

"I'm not a warrior, Firas," Jaufre said by way of explanation for the ignorance and ineptitude he was about to display. "I'm a trader."

"You carry a sword," the havildar said, unsurprised at this unsolicited confidence. "Sooner or later, someone will force you to use it." He hesitated, and then said, very gently, "You could lay it aside, young sir."

Jaufre had unbuckled the scabbard from about his chest and now he frowned down at it and the sword it sheathed. He looked up to meet Johanna's eyes. She said nothing, only waited for him to choose.

He drew his father's sword, handed her belt and scabbard, and turned. He thought he saw a trace of approval in the havildar's eyes, but later he would be equally certain he had imagined it. The havildar's approval was not so easily won.

"Yours is a weapon of the West," Firas pacing around him, hands clasped behind his back. "The Western warrior prefers a straight blade for hacking through heavy armor, wielded from horseback." He stopped to draw his own weapon. "My scimitar is of the East, also meant to be used from horseback, but shorter and used against a lightly-armored opponent, usually after the opponent's line has been weakened by archers."

He tossed Jaufre his scimitar. Jaufre caught it, just, in his left hand. "You will notice the difference in weight."

Jaufre tested both swords, and his eyebrows went up.

Firas nodded. "One on one, your sword will have the advantage."

"Until I meet someone with a longer sword," Jaufre said.

"Until then." Firas held up an admonitory finger. "You will have the advantage, that is, once you learn to use it properly. An untrained soldier is more of a hazard to himself than he is to anyone else."

After Jaufre had nearly cut off his own hand and had gashed his own cheek, he took the havildar's warning more seriously.

But that would be in the future. This morning Firas had caused a thick post to be buried deep in the sand, and had Jaufre hack at it with a wooden practice sword, forehand and backhand, over and over, again and again, until Jaufre's arms felt as if they would fall off. "This post is buried behind the cook tents at each of our camps," the havildar said. "Half of each practice session will be spent at it."

Jaufre, sweat rolling down his face, the muscles in his arms burning, gasped out something that passed for, "Yes, havildar."

Firas then had Jaufre switch to his own sword and walk through a series of different movements, cut, thrust, parry, and right, left and overhead variations. There wasn't much finesse to it, as Jaufre soon came to realize. A sword was essentially a club with an edge.

Firas walked through each movement slowly, standing next to Jaufre and commanding him to mirror his own movements. Then he stepped opposite Jaufre and repeated those movements, meeting them with his own in mirror image.

After the work with the post, it was all Jaufre could do to get his sword to shoulder height, and Firas took advantage of every gap in his defenses, usually with a hard rap with the side of his blade on whatever portion of Jaufre's anatomy was convenient. There were many such gaps.

At some point during the following year, Firas stepped back and dropped his sword. "Enough for your first lesson, I think."

Jaufre blinked the sweat from his eyes and looked around to find that many of Uncle Cheng's guard had assembled in a circle. There were smiles hidden and smiles not and much nudging of elbows. Johanna, standing a little apart with her hands clasped over the sword's sheath as if she were praying, watched them with a face wiped unusually clean of expression.

"Tomorrow at the same time, young sir?" Firas said, producing a length of cloth and wiping his blade.

Jaufre took a deep breath and with trembling arms brought up his father's sword and wiped it on the edge of his tunic. He made a silent vow to acquire a clean cloth for cleansing his blade before their next practice. "Tomorrow," he said. It was all he could manage.

Firas inclined his head, a ghost of a smile on his face. "Until then."

Johanna, mercifully, waited until they were well away from the practice yard. "Where does it hurt?"

"Everywhere," he said. He'd meant it to be a shout but it came out as more of a groan.

She nodded, her suspicion confirmed. "Perhaps another visit to the baths."

It was good advice, despite its source, and he took it. He was marginally mobile when he awoke that evening, only to be nearly incapable of helping strike their yurt afterward. Johanna and Shasha broke their camp without comment, although there were meaningful looks. The night that followed, spent on camelback, was sheer agony.

Uncle Cheng at first skirted the Taklamakan Desert to the north, stopping at oasis towns and trading as they went. Shasha purchased cakes of indigo dye which she said would profit them well in Antioch and Acre, where they could buy kermes or carmine dye for trading farther west. Johanna found a merchant who specialized in antiquities and acquired a dozen flying horses made of bronze, all small, exquisitely made and of a portable size.

"Those aren't Han," Jaufre said.

"Who west of Kashgar will know that?" Johanna said. Her fingers caressed the mane of one of the horses. "And they are lovely little pieces in their own right. Who wouldn't pay a handsome sum to display one of these in their public rooms, to the envy of their neighbors and friends?" Her eyes took on a faraway look. "Perhaps I should find a marble carver. We could double the price if each one included its own pedestal."

"And it would be no strain at all on our pack animals to ask them to carry marble pedestals in addition to the solid bronze statues," Jaufre said cordially.

Shasha watched Johanna flounce off. Jaufre flapped a hand at Shasha's raised eyebrow and hobbled off in the opposite direction.

The feelings generated by discovery of the contents of Johanna's purse were prone to display themselves at odd moments. Shasha sighed and kept her inevitable thoughts to herself.

Jaufre's weapons training continued apace. The first morning he was able to block all of the havildar's blows, Firas introduced him to the shield, and then the mace, and then the flail, and then the axe, and then the lance. New muscles he didn't even know he had set up their individual protests. At which point Firas, obviously close kin to Father John's Christian devil, set the better swordsmen among the guards to attack Jaufre without warning, so that Jaufre found himself on alert at every moment of the night or day. Before long he was able to come out of a sound sleep, on his feet with his father's sword in his hand, and beat off an attack in the blazing sun of midday.

Johanna and Shasha, woken during the same attack, knew enough not to waste their breath in complaints, and perfected a quick roll to the wall of the yurt, beneath it and out, while the battle raged within.

None of the surprise attacks were half-hearted. One evening, as the caravan was being loaded and the camels were coming reluctantly to their feet, Jaufre blocked one of the havildar's thrusts and pushed through to touch the point of his blade to the havildar's tunic. He dropped his sword and stood back.

Firas, to Jaufre's infinite and inarticulate pride, saluted Jaufre with his scimitar. "You improve, young sir. You improve."

Félicien wrote a song about it and sang it at the campfire that night to loud acclaim. Jaufre's aches and pains lessened. When they were near a city he sought out the hot baths. When they camped in caravansaries or on the trail Shasha rubbed him down with oil, strong fingers kneading at the hard knots of muscles bunched beneath his skin. After a while he had to find a seamstress to let out the shoulders and sleeves of his tunics.

One morning he was already laying face down on his bed, shirtless, his head pillowed in his arms, half asleep. He heard the flap of the yurt rustle and said sleepily, "Shasha?"

She didn't answer, and there was a long silence. Then her knees dropped next to him and he heard her rub oil into her hands. She laid those hands on his back and he knew instantly that they did not belong to the wise woman. They were strong, vigorous hands that kneaded the tension from his muscles every bit as capably as Shasha's would have, but instead of a massage this felt like a caress, like a prelude to love. He shifted when his body reacted, but he was anything but uncomfortable. He had wanted her for so long now, and for so long she had been unable to see anything but a brother when she looked at him.

He rolled to his back and looked up at her. Her hands had dropped to her thighs and her eyes were wide, tracing the curve of muscle and bone from his shoulder to his chest. His eyes followed the trail of golden down over his abdomen, and widened. She looked up at his face, startled. He made no attempt to hide what he was feeling.

Her lips parted and she leaned a little forward, and Shasha came into the yurt, oblivious to the tension, or making a good show of it. "Ah, good, Johanna, I see you've eased the pain of our wounded warrior."

Not quite, Jaufre thought.

Shasha, meantime, had her own agenda. The following morning after they pitched the yurt she drew the younger woman to one side. "Do you remember the herbs I gave you before you went to Edyk?"

Johanna colored. "Yes."

"You took them?"

"I did. Steeped in hot water every morning, as you instructed. They tasted terrible."

"Most effective medicines do, unfortunately. Edyk didn't object?"

"Edyk didn't know." Johanna looked away. "I made sure he was deep asleep each time."

"Good." Shasha nodded. "Good. You are pleased to be without child?"

Johanna was silent. Traveling the Road, having adventures, seeing all that there was to see, finding her grandfather, these were the things she was looking forward to.

Still, to have had Edyk's child…would have been most inconvenient. She didn't need a child to remember him by. Perhaps she would marry and have children one day, although that day was visible only through a rosy cloud in the distant future, with the father of said children an even less distinct figure. "Yes," she said firmly. "I didn't thank you, Shasha. I am very grateful."

"Good," Shasha said briskly, "then you will not object to learning to make your own." She led the way to a blanket she had spread behind their yurt, her herbs set out in small neat bags made of muslin, each marked with a Mandarin character. She sat down tailor fashion and motioned Johanna to join her. "This is pennyroyal," she said. "Take a pinch. Smell it. Taste it, a very little. When I find some of it growing I'll show you."

Dutifully Johanna pinched, smelled, tasted.

"This is mugwort," Shasha said, offering another muslin bag. She waited as Johanna went through the ritual. "Take either one dram of the pennyroyal, or one dram of the mugwort, but never both." She shook out a portion of the pennyroyal into her palm, demonstrating the amount. "Add one teaspoon of blue cohash. Infuse the herbs in one cup of boiling water and drink. Twice a day for six days, no more."

"And this will—"

The two women looked at one another, united in the eternal female conspiracy against the burden placed on them by nature. "Will bring on a delayed menstruation," Shasha said, without expression. "You must pay attention, Johanna. If you are a week or less late, take the potion as prescribed. If it does not bring on your menses, Johanna, if it does not—" she emphasized those last words "—you must not repeat the dosage, do you understand? You must not. It could lead to uncontrolled bleeding. You could bleed to death."

Johanna took a deep breath. "I understand. But why tell me now? Edyk is five hundred leagues behind us."

Shasha was packing up her herbs. "There are other men in the world, Johanna." Her hands stilled and she looked up. "One in our own yurt."

Johanna went instantly scarlet, leapt to her feet and marched off.

# · Thirteen ·

*Kuche to Kashgar*

⊢———⊣

Firas' chief asset for the job of havildar, so far as Jaufre could see, was the ability to instill fear into his subordinates. "Why do they fear?" Johanna said, sensibly, and Jaufre spent a few evenings loitering around the guards' campfire, participating in soft boxing competitions and wrestling matches and archery contests and taking care not to win all the time. "He's a Nazari Ismaili," he reported back.

Johanna and Shasha looked blank.

"From Alamut," Jaufre said.

Recognition dawned. "He's an Assassin?" Johanna said, thrilled. "Really? I've never met an Assassin before."

"Yes, well, try not to sound so delighted," Jaufre said dryly. "You may not have met one now. That sect died out over a hundred years ago. Or was wiped out, more like."

Johanna's brow puckered. "But Father said that Grandfather visited the Mountain, and might even have met the Old Man."

"Your grandfather wasn't always the most reliable source, as the honorable Wu Li himself admitted," Shasha said.

After that Johanna made a point of watching Firas at work when she could. She detected no outward menace in his demeanor, but he did have an indefinable presence that inspired respect, if not, as Jaufre claimed, fear in his subordinates. When he issued an order, it was followed, promptly and without question, and without his ever having to lay a hand on the hilt of the curved sword he wore at his side, much less drawing it from its sturdy leather scabbard.

"What were you hoping for," Jaufre said one evening, "that he'd kill someone right in front of you so you could see the gold dagger of the Assassin in action?"

Johanna put up her nose at his and Shasha's laughter.

From Kuche, Uncle Cheng had sniffed the horizon for weather and found it mild for the season, and so they crossed the Taklamakan to Yarkent at a brisk march that had them arriving in record time. There, Shasha traded nearly everything but the Mien rubies in their hems for spices, peppercorns from Malabar, nutmeg from the Moluccas, cinnamon from Java the Less, cloves from Ceylon.

When Johanna mourned the loss of the sables out loud Shasha held up a canvas packet, no larger than Jaufre's fist, plump with vanilla beans from Madagascar. "The annual salary for a Mosul doctor."

No more was said. Spices were small and light, and when Shasha was done two of their half dozen camels were packed to the saddle horns with the aromatic cargo. "The farther west we travel, the more valuable these will become," she said with satisfaction.

Uncle Cheng, too, was pleased. The risky desert journey had paid off in excellent profit for all, and the usual grumblings any caravan master heard daily had been replaced by smug smiles and fat purses.

They had been on the road ninety days, only seventeen of those days given over to trading, one day extra in Kuche for the races and their aftermath, the rest in motion. Uncle Cheng had pushed them hard but the journey had paid off in goods traded to their advantage. As they approached the walls of Kashgar the rubies of Mien remained securely sewn into their hems.

There had been no further attacks upon their yurt. They had glimpsed small groups of what they presumed to be raiders on distant hilltops, and the three of them might have had their suspicions about who might be with those menacing groups, but the size of the caravan and the number of guards had been enough of a discouragement, at least so far.

What happened after Kashgar was another story, one Jaufre worried over. They left their pack animals under Uncle Cheng's capable eye, mounted horse and donkey (Félicien accompanied them) and spurred ahead to arrive at the great east gate of the city two hours in advance of the rest of the caravan.

Which was where Johanna acquired her monk.

He was being beaten with a stick outside the gates, in a formally appointed punishment complete with magistrate, drum and enthusiastic crowd. The stick was large and smooth from much use. The strokes were slow and measured and delivered with the full force of the arm of a man as large and muscular as the convicted felon was small and thin. The man with the stick was stripped to the waist and sweating with effort. So was the drummer, a slender boy of ten who watched his stick rather than the flogger's.

The felon was also stripped to the waist, displaying a torso with barely enough flesh to cover his bones. His hair was black and raggedly cut, his skin a pale gold.

Johanna reined in, she could not herself have said why. Perforce, Jaufre and Shasha reined in next to her. Taken by surprise, Félicien had to haul back on the reins of his donkey who, recognizing the walls of the city as housing food, water and rest was reluctant to stop until he was inside them. He finally acquiesced in this change of plan, not without protesting bawls.

Johanna waited a decent time before addressing herself to the magistrate, an elderly, impassive man attired in the flowing robe of his office. His head was shaven, and two long, thin mustaches trailed down each side of his thick, sternly set lips. By not so much as the twitch of an eyebrow did he betray that he knew perfectly well whose daughter she was.

She knew him as well as he knew her, but she took her cue from his formal manner. "Greetings, honored one," she said. She spoke in Mandarin and received a blank stare. She repeated her greeting in Mongol.

"Greetings, lady," the magistrate replied in that language. "You are welcome."

"We have traveled far and seek a meal, a bath and a bed within your walls this night."

"There are many such within the walls of Kashgar."

"It is good to know. We have been many days on the road, and are tired and hungry." Johanna and the magistrate watched the stick descend again. "Perhaps, honored one, you would know of an inn where we might find cleanliness and comfort."

"All inns within the walls of Kashgar are clean and comfortable," the magistrate said, "but it is well known that the Inn of the Green Dragon bakes the finest naan in the city and airs its blankets twice-monthly."

"I thank you, honored one. To the Green Dragon we will go." But she made no effort to leave.

They watched the beating go on in silence for a moment. Félicien gave Shasha a questioning look. Shasha rolled her eyes in reply.

"What has this old man done, honored one," Johanna said, "that he should be punished so severely?"

The official gave a mournful shake of his head. "He has represented himself as a holy man, and accepted alms from the citizens of Kashgar. The law requires that such a one be beaten once for each alm."

Johanna lowered her eyes to show her respect and said, "Truly, a just and equitable law, worthy of the rulers of such a great city."

The magistrate bowed slightly, accepting the compliment. Twice more the stick was raised and lowered against the man's shrinking back.

"He is not holy, then?"

The magistrate shrugged. "He drinks sulphur and quicksilver once a day. He says he is a hundred and fifty years old. This may make him holy in the city of Calicut, but not in the city of Kashgar."

The stick rose and fell. At last Johanna said, "It is not for this unworthy one to suggest such a punishment is unmerited, yet I have pity for the old man. Is there no way to redeem this sinner to the path of righteousness?"

The magistrate was silent. At last he said, "There is one way. If the offender be able to ransom himself by paying nine times the value of the thing stolen, he is freed and released from further punishment."

Another stroke fell.

"And nine times the value of the thing stolen is what, in this instance, honored one?"

The magistrate folded his hands beneath his sleeves and regarded his shoes, the toes of which were pointed, curled and embroidered with gold thread. "How can one value the honor of a city?" he said piously, and

Johanna knew at once that it was going to be expensive. "This charlatan has trespassed on the faith of our citizens, has stolen the very trust out of their hearts. Fifty rials."

Johanna and the magistrate regarded the old man's bleeding back together in silence. "He seems such a little, insignificant man to have caused any great harm to a city as exalted as Kashgar," Johanna said finally. "But it is as you say, honored one, that where one offends, one should atone for one's crimes. Ten rials."

The embroidered toes of the magistrate's shoes raised as he rocked back on his heels in shock. "This charlatan has trespassed on the faith of our citizens," he said indignantly. "He has stolen the veneration and obedience due our own ordained priesthood. Forty."

"Twenty, and we will take him with us when we leave."

The magistrate watched two more blows fall. "It is done," he said. "Release him."

The man wielding the stick cut the thongs that bound the old man to the post. The boy with the drum looked relieved. The crowd was disappointed, and there were some rumbles of discontent and some dark glances cast their way.

Shasha slid down from her horse and reached for her basket of herbs. The old man warded her off with one hand and took three trembling, determined steps forward to stand in front of Johanna. "You have done me service," he said in solemn if unpracticed Mandarin.

Stooping, he touched one finger to a pile of dry cow dung, straightened, and reached up to touch that finger to Johanna's forehead. North Wind danced a little in place, his refined nostrils offended by the smell coming off the old man. Johanna soothed him with a pat and the old man repeated the procedure with Jaufre, Shasha and Félicien, and then, pressing his hands together beneath his chin, bowed to each in turn. "I thank you."

Johanna, repressing a strong urge to reach for the nearest water sack, bowed in return. "You are welcome, old man." She indicated an old scar on his left cheek. "I see you bear the mark of the Khan. For what were you imprisoned?"

The old man smiled faintly. "Practicing religion without a license."

Shasha snorted. Jaufre raised one eyebrow. "You seem to make a habit of that, old man," Johanna said. "If we lend you our countenance and company in the days ahead, would it be possible for you to confine your activities to reflection and meditation?" She glanced at the magistrate. "At least until we are out of reach of the long arm of Kashgari justice?"

The old man inclined his head without answering and with unusual tact Johanna forbore to press him for a more definite answer. His face was without color and his golden skin seemed painted on over his high brow and cheekbones. "Very well, old man, you are welcome in our company. Will you take supper with us?"

"At the Inn of the Green Dragon?"

"How did you know?"

The old man shrugged. "You are strangers looking for lodging. You spoke with the magistrate. The magistrate's mother-in-law's brother owns the Inn of the Green Dragon."

Johanna repressed a smile. It was what one expected, after all. She would go to the inn and pay for a night's lodging for the group and then spend that night in the caravansary with Wu Cheng as usual. "May one know your name, old man?"

The old man smiled for the first time. "Call me Hari," he said, and fainted at North Wind's feet.

Shasha knelt beside him, saying practically, "The best thing that could happen. Jaufre, open the basket and hand me the packet marked 'Alukrese.'" She rolled a large pinch of dried leaves between her palms and let them sift down over the old man's torn back. "That will stop the bleeding and keep the wounds free from infection. When we get to the caravansary I will give him ground willow bark for the pain and valerian to put him to sleep."

"Will he be ready to travel by the time we leave?"

Shasha shrugged. "Who can say? That one—" indicating the receding back of the magistrate "—would have him so, and unless we want a taste of the stick for ourselves, it would be wise if he were." She covered the old man's back with a clean cloth and bound it lightly. She sat back on her heels and looked up at Johanna. "Why are we rescuing him, by the way?"

Johanna contemplated the face lying at her breast, lines smoothed from his brow and the corners of his mouth in unconsciousness. He looked much younger asleep than he did awake. Certainly nowhere near a hundred and fifty years old. "I like his face."

Shasha looked at Jaufre and rolled her eyes again. Jaufre shrugged.

They bore the old man to the caravansary while Johanna went in search of the Inn of the Green Dragon. She handed over an exorbitant fee for rooms she had no intention of occupying, accepted a piece of undercooked naan that she threw to the dogs, and arrived at the caravansary at the same time as Uncle Cheng.

"Ho!" he said upon seeing her. "You have picked up another stray, I see."

"She makes a habit of picking up strays?" Félicien said.

Shasha and Jaufre looked at each other, and then looked at him.

"Oh," he said.

They woke the next morning to find the monk sitting before the uncurtained window of their common room, directly in the rays of the sun, with his feet crossed on his lap and his hands palm up on his knees. He was humming, a deep, not unpleasant sound like the buzzing of a safely distant hive of bees. "Brahman is. Brahman is the door. Om is the glory of Brahman."

He continued to hum as they moved around him, elongating the oms into drawn-out syllables that lasted the length of a breath, which for Hari was very long, the m's seeming to vibrate against the very walls of the room. All of them were Mongol enough, at least by association, to have respect for holy men no matter to which god they bowed their head. After all, if the god graced Hari with good fortune, he might have a little left over for them.

When they were ready to leave, the humming ceased. He opened his eyes and smiled at Shasha. "By the vision of Sankhya and the harmony of Yoga a man knows God, and when a man knows God he is free from all fetters. I thank you for your care of me, mistress. I have rested well, and I am ready to start." He looked at Johanna. "Where are we going?"

"West, old man, as far as we can go and not fall off the edge of the world," Johanna said. "But we do not go for a few days yet."

The old man considered this in silence. "It is my life's work," he said at last, "to seek out new places, and the people who live there, and discover how and to whom they give their faith."

"Are you on a pilgrimage, then, old man?" Jaufre said.

"A pilgrimage?" The monk savored the word. "I am a seeker after truth, young master, wherever I may find it."

"So long as you do not seek after trouble at the same time," Shasha said.

"Trouble, mistress?" The monk looked amazed, as if he were not the one sitting there with the marks of a severe beating all over his back.

"Not your best idea," Shasha told Johanna.

"We will bring food and water," Johanna told the old man. "For now, it would be best if you kept to this room. Eat, drink, rest, sleep. Heal. Be certain you wish to join with us. Our journey will not be a short or easy one."

"No worthwhile journey ever is," the monk said, and formed his thumbs and forefingers into circles, closed his eyes, and began again to om.

On the street Jaufre said, "I will meet you at Uncle Cheng's fire tonight."

Johanna and Shasha watched him walk down the bustling street and vanish from sight around a corner, and proceeded on their way without conversation. They both knew where he was going.

When the pearl trade had increased, their trips had taken them more often east than west, and trips to Kashgar had decreased to one every two or three years. But no matter how long the time between visits, Jaufre never failed to ask for news of his mother in the souks and slave markets of the town. There had never been any word.

The two women wandered the market with purpose, looking for old friends, introducing themselves to new ones. Yusuf the oil seller had died the previous year and had been succeeded by his son Malik, who was desolated to hear of Wu Li's death. Son and daughter shared a half hour of gentle reminiscence that made them both feel better over their losses.

Shasha found a buyer for their cinnamon but his price was not high enough. "We will do better to wait for Tabriz, or Gaza."

"Or even Venice," Johanna said.

"Indeed," Shasha said, her voice very dry.

The livestock pens were thin, the herds not yet down from the summer pastures, but horses there were in plenty, and Johanna passed the word that she might have a nag with enough breath in him to stagger around a racecourse, provided it was a short one. This challenge was accepted in much the spirit it was given, and before long in their perambulations through the city they began to hear the rumor of a horse race the following day, and of a challenger to perennial favorite Blue Sky come new out of the east, prepared to lay waste to all comers.

"A formidable foe, it would seem," Johanna said gravely the third time they heard this tale. "Has anyone seen this challenger?"

"Oh yes, miss." The fruit seller, who was probably a tout on the side on race days, was anxious to assure her, and himself of her future bet. "Black as the night and fleet as the shooting star across the skies. Blue Sky has met his match."

"That is fast indeed," Johanna said. "I should definitely place a bet, then."

"Indeed you should, young miss. The odds on Blue Sky—"

"Yes, but I think I shall put my money on this unknown, black, did you say? Someone should, don't you think? To encourage future challengers. Otherwise who will dare to race against the formidable Blue Sky?" She placed her bet, paid for their oranges and moved on.

That evening when they met at Uncle Cheng's fire, Johanna met Jaufre's eyes. He shook his head, once, and she dropped her own so he would not see the sympathy there. Jaufre didn't want sympathy, he wanted news of his mother, and his bleak expression was enough to tell her that none of the slave dealers in the city had been able or willing to oblige.

The next day North Wind raced, and won. Johanna collected her winnings from the fruit seller, who gave her a wounded look but nobly did not complain, at least not within her hearing.

Sheik Mohammed met her as she led North Wind to his picket. She felt Jaufre stiffen next to her, only to be waved off by the sheik. "I renew my offer to purchase your horse," he said. "Again, name your price."

"He is not for sale," Johanna said. She was growing a little weary of the sheik. "Not for any price."

The sheik regarded her, his face as immobile as ever. "I could take him from you."

She laughed, and stepped to one side. "By all means. Try."

The sheik hesitated, and stepped forward to lay a hand on North Wind's halter.

North Wind met his hand with his teeth, closing them around his wrist. His two guards came fully alert, and this time it was Jaufre's turn to wave them down. "Johanna," he said, resigned.

Johanna smacked her hand against North Wind's side, and the great white horse rolled an eye in her direction, seemed to conduct an inward debate, and then almost with a sigh released the sheik.

He examined his wrist. Apart from some slobber and the red indent of North Wind's excellent teeth, it was intact. "I would speak with you," he said to Jaufre.

"If it's about North Wind—"

"It is, but it is not a subject I may discuss with a woman."

Johanna, fitting a curry brush over her hand, raised a shoulder in answer to Jaufre's raised eyebrow.

Out of earshot the sheik said, "Will she allow North Wind to breed with one of my mares?"

Jaufre grinned. "For a fee, I'm sure she would."

In the end North Wind bred with three mares over their last three days in Kashgar, two gleaming equine Arabian princesses belonging to the sheik and a third older mare belonging to a Kashgari noble.

"Honorable niece," Uncle Cheng said over their last dinner together, "you know that that horse will be a lure to every thief and robber and brigand from here to Antioch."

"They might try to steal him, uncle," she said, scooping up two fingers full of a delicious lamb pilaf cooked with plums. She licked her fingers and smiled at Jaufre. "But North Wind has a mind of his own, and formidable defenses. Even if they could steal him, I doubt very much that they will be able to keep him."

A circle formed soon after that, and the singing began. Johanna fetched the Robe of a Thousand Larks, mended with invisible stitches by Shasha's patient hands, and sang when her turn came. Jaufre, a pleasant baritone, provided a solid base note and Shasha and even Uncle Cheng made a pleasing counterpoint hum. Félicien joined in on the last stanza and then took his own turn, beginning with a song about a large white horse with fleet hooves and a nasty disposition that had everyone roaring and joining in on the chorus.

The sheik was there, not singing, and the sheik's son, looking as if he wished he could. His eyes strayed rather too often in Johanna's direction for Jaufre's taste. Johanna saw neither of their glances. Shasha watched them both from the corner of her eye, and then Firas joined them and raised a surprising baritone in a warrior's song, all clashing swords and thumping shields and wives and children left behind. The chorus, booming, rhythmic, sounded like an army on the march.

They sang until the moon rose, bright enough to cast shadows on the rugs covering the sand of the caravansary. They sang as it set, the shadows elongating into weird shapes that seemed to move with a life of their own.

As she sang Johanna looked at the windows of the apartments that ringed the second floor. She had stayed in all of them at one time or another, her mother and father in the next room, Shasha always in the bedroll next to her, Jaufre across the door, his chosen spot wherever they stayed. Her heart ached in her breast and tears filled her eyes. She blinked them away and returned full-throated to the song, a tale of a housewife, a tinker and a wronged husband.

The moon set on one horizon as faint golden light grew on another. Groups began to say their goodbyes and retire to their rooms and their yurts. Uncle Cheng sent for his teapot and poured for them all. The dark, fragrant brew was smooth and satisfying on the tongue. "Enjoy it while you can," Uncle Cheng said. "They don't drink tea in the West."

"Then we will introduce it to them," the irrepressible Johanna said.

"And make a profit on it," Jaufre said, and surprised, Johanna laughed with him, invulnerable and immortal in their youth.

Uncle Cheng sighed to himself. "You will trade as you go?"

"Yes, uncle."

"You have the names?"

"Grigori in Kabul, Hasan in Tabriz, Fakhir in Antioch, Eneas in Alexandria, Soranzo in Gaza." She touched the leather purse at her waist, and returned a grin to Shasha's glare.

Uncle Cheng noted the byplay without comment. Wise old Uncle Cheng knew her well enough to harbor his own suspicions. "And you have enough funds to be going on with?"

"More than enough, uncle." She didn't reach for the hems of her robe and trousers, just. "Father provided for us well." This time she didn't look at Shasha.

"Good." Wu Cheng nodded. "Good. I have a few more names you may find useful." He smiled. "And a bale of green tea to comfort you on your journey, and—" he turned to beckon to a servant, who brought forward a large bundle "—these." He unwrapped the bundle to reveal coats of black Astrachan lamb, fully lined with raw silk and fastened with black shell buttons and a sash of black brocade. Each coat fit beautifully, obviously tailor-made on Uncle Cheng's instructions. "Uncle," Johanna said. "I don't know what to say."

Jaufre stood very straight, the coat fitting him like a second skin, the black of the curly astrakhan highlighting the blue of his eyes and the gold of his hair. "It is a gift worthy of a prince, uncle," he said.

Uncle Cheng waved off their thanks. "It was Wu Li's choice to venture not beyond Kashgar, but often have I crossed the Pamir, and always, always have I been colder than a widow's—"

Shasha cleared her throat.

"Well," Cheng said. "Very, very cold." He looked at each of them in turn. "It will not be an easy journey."

Johanna thought of Hari, the mad monk, who she fancied she could hear omming from their rooms. "No worthwhile journey ever is, uncle."

Uncle Cheng laughed and shook his head.

Firas, still sitting with them, cleared his throat. "Wu Cheng."

Something close to a wince crossed the older man's face, as if he thought he knew what was coming and didn't relish it. "Firas."

"It has been my great honor to serve you these past two years," Firas said.

Wu Cheng sighed. "And your service has been more than satisfactory, havildar."

Firas bent his head. "I thank you, Wu Cheng, for that testimonial." He turned to Johanna and Jaufre but seemed to be speaking to Shasha. "You have heard your uncle speak well of me. It is my wish to return to the West. I wonder if my company on the Road would be acceptable to you, so long as our paths lie together."

"Why?" Johanna said, blunt as ever.

"Perhaps I do not wish to leave a task half done," he said, with a slight bow in Jaufre's direction.

Johanna looked skeptical.

"Perhaps I have been long enough in the east, and wish to return to the land of my birth," he said.

"The Old Man is dead and his people are dispersed to the four corners of Persia," Jaufre said.

"And I am one of them," the havildar said without resentment.

Johanna and Jaufre exchanged a quick glance, and as one they looked to Shasha. "Shu Shao?" Jaufre said. "What is your opinion in this matter?"

Shasha took her time, regarding her loosely clasped hands. "Why," she said lightly, "that Firas of Alamut is a man of good reputation and equable temperament, and a capable havildar as vouched for by the honorable Wu Cheng and as witnessed by each of us these past ninety days, and should be a welcome addition to our party."

"I thank you, Shu Shao," Firas said.

"He has left me a capable second-in-command," Uncle Cheng said. "And truly, my children, I will feel easier in my mind with Firas as your guide. He is quite deadly with that blade, you know."

Jaufre knew, but Johanna was still unsatisfied, until she intercepted a look that the havildar, unaware that he was being observed, gave Shasha. "Is Firas in love with Shasha?" she whispered to Jaufre.

He looked startled. "I don't know. Why?"

"I saw him look at her."

"Oh well, that clinches it."

"Jaufre, I tell you, it was that kind of look!"

He gave her a look of his own, and leaned in close. "Are you quite sure you would recognize a look of that kind if you saw one?"

Her lips parted as she stared up at him, and he heard with satisfaction her breath catch in her throat.

Félicien struck a jubilant chord that startled everyone and said, "I myself am on a westward trajectory. Might I join you as well?"

This had not been so entirely unexpected. Jaufre smiled and Johanna grinned, and the sun tipped over the horizon, flooding the courtyard with light. Cattle lowed, camels groaned, and North Wind sent out in inquiring whinny that had Johanna on her feet and running to him. She returned in time to see the brighter stars begin to fade from existence, as savory odors began drifting toward them from the cook fire. Outside the walls, they could hear the city of Kashgar coming slowly awake.

Uncle Cheng stirred. "I must tell you a story, before we part."

"Naturally," Shasha said, casting her eyes upward.

"Yes, yes, I know," Wu Cheng said with unusual asperity, "the fat old man blathering on yet again to no purpose." He glared at her, and then at Jaufre, who sat up straight and felt guilty, although he couldn't have said why.

"You are setting out on a wonderful adventure, agreed," Uncle Cheng said, turning to Johanna, and the reproof in his eyes stilled the indulgent smile on her lips. "Why shouldn't you? You're young, you have strong bodies and sound minds. Like many young people, you crave new experiences, excitement, adventure. Not for you a safe life at home, I understand that, and thanks to Wu Li's fine example you are well versed in matters of trade. I have no fear that you will go hungry, no matter how far you travel or where your journey ends." He brooded for a moment.

"But I would tell you a story nonetheless. A cautionary tale, so that you do not go heedless into the west." He smoothed his palms over his trousers. "This story I heard long since, of a man and a time even longer past. He lived in Alexandria, oh, five hundred years ago and more. He was Muslim, and his name was Cosmas."

Jaufre leaned back against a saddle and Johanna, without thinking, leaned against him in the way she always had.

"It is said that this Cosmas constructed a model of the earth, in the shape of a large, rectangular box with a high, curved lid. The lid represented heaven, and as man would look down on it, so would God look down on his work. Do you see it?"

"I see it, uncle."

"Inside the chest there was a great mountain, and around this mountain moved the sun. Because the mountain was uneven in size and shape, the rays of the sun shining down upon the earth shifted as the sun moved, making the days and the seasons unequal in length."

"Was heaven in the box?"

"There was Paradise," Uncle Cheng said. "From Paradise flowed four great rivers, the Indus into India, the Nile through Egypt, the Tigris and Euphrates to Mesopotamia. There were four peoples in Cosmas' world, the Scythians in the north, the Indians in the East, the Ethiops in the south, and the Celts in the west."

Johanna waited. When Cheng said no more, she said, "But where was Everything Under the Heavens?"

Wu Cheng looked at her, his expression sober. "It wasn't in the chest."

Johanna sat up. "Not in the box? Why not?"

"I don't know why not."

Johanna was unbelieving. "Was this Cosmas unaware of the existence of Everything Under the Heavens?"

Wu Cheng considered. "He may have been. He may also have been ignoring it, deliberately so."

"But how can this be?" Johanna said. "One cannot ignore Everything Under the Heavens. It just…is. Everything Under the Heavens, is, well, Everything Under the Heavens."

"Not everything," Cheng said. "Not even most."

Johanna didn't understand him, and didn't understand Cosmas, either, for that matter. "And to make the earth a box when everyone knows it is a ball? This is nonsense, Uncle."

"It is," Cheng agreed. "And then it isn't."

She looked at him accusingly. "You're as bad as Shasha, uncle."

"I am wounded that you would say so," he said gravely.

Shasha snorted.

"Johanna." The serious note in Wu Cheng's voice caused Johanna's smile to fade. He looked stern, even a little harsh. "Jaufre, yes, even you, Shasha, listen to me. If the Celts and the Scythians and the Indians and the Ethiops think they share the whole world between them, and if they have thought that for five hundred years, and if for that long they have ignored the existence of Everything Under the Heavens…"

"Then," Jaufre said, "they will not wish to hear of the power and the greatness that we have left behind."

"No. They are also very jealous of their gods. You would do well to adopt, outwardly at least, whatever faith rules wherever you are."

Johanna thought of Hari, the monk at present eating their food and sleeping in a bed they had provided him, enjoying a freedom purchased by them. She had been ready to leave Everything Under the Heavens since she was old enough to walk, but for the first time she began to realize the dangers of doing so.

"Have you given any thought to where you will go?" Uncle Cheng said. "Other than simply west. Baghdad and Hormuz are not what they once were. Tabriz, perhaps?"

Johanna, Jaufre and Shasha exchanged glances. Jaufre would have said, Anywhere I might find word of my mother. Shasha would have said, As far away from the fell hand of the Widow Wu as possible. Johanna said, "Tabriz, certainly. Wu Li said my grandfather called Tabriz a crossroads of commerce. Then Gaza, perhaps. From Gaza we could take ship to Venice."

"You don't want to stop in Byzantium?" Jaufre said.

"Most of what was worth seeing in Byzantium," Uncle Cheng said, "is now in Venice."

# · Fourteen ·

*Kashgar and the Pamir*

⊢——⊣

"Kerman?" Hari repeated. "In Kerman, unless the merchants be well armed they run the risk of being murdered, or at least robbed."

"Have you been there, old man?" Jaufre said.

The monk shook his head. "I have not, master. But I have traveled the road from India, and I have heard this said of Kerman many times. And before Kerman," he said dreamily, "I have heard of the plain of Pamir—so lofty and cold that you do not often see birds fly. Because of this great cold, fire does not burn so brightly, nor give out so much heat as usual, nor does it cook food so efficiently."

"Are you sure you want to come with us?" Shasha said pointedly.

He smiled at her. "Of course. Let us follow the chariot of Arjuna, whose wheels are right effort and whose driver is truth. Thus shall we all come to the land which is free from fear."

"Kerman, then," Jaufre said, bringing them back to the point. "The carpets there are said to be very fine."

"And Tabriz afterward," Shasha said.

"And then Gaza," Johanna said, and gave an impish smile. "And anything in between that looks interesting."

Firas and Félicien were interested auditors but contributed no opinions.

"Johanna?"

Johanna looked up to see Fatima standing in the doorway, an even more joyous smile than usual on her face. "Azar is here."

A slim young man in pants and tunic with a dark blue cheche

wrapped about his head stood next to her, a shy smile on his face. He was older and taller than when they had seen him last, but then they all were, and they had no trouble recognizing her betrothed.

"Azar!" Jaufre leaped to his feet and they clasped hands warmly. Shasha pushed him to one side and took Azar by his shoulders. "You look well," she said, and gave him a gentle shake. She was displaced in turn by Johanna, who gave him a hearty embrace. He colored slightly, but he was definitely pleased to see them.

"We are coming with you to Kerman!" Fatima said.

Johanna was startled. "We only just decided we were going there."

Fatima gave that remark the back of her hand. "Father has heard of a new kind of grain available in the west, one that in the right climate can bear twice in the same season."

"Has Ahmed the baker become a grain merchant, then?"

"Who cares, so long as our time together is not yet done? Although—" Fatima managed to assume a stern expression "—we are not pitching our yurt anywhere near yours again. I tremble to think what would happen the next time you called on the North Wind for aid."

The four of them laughed.

Uncle Cheng had arranged for them to join a caravan headed for Kerman by way of Talikan, where they would trade for almonds and pistachios but mostly for salt. "It is said there are mountains of it," Jaufre said.

"What's so special about this particular salt?" Johanna said.

"It is said to be washed in the azure waves of the Gulf of Persia, and harvested by virgins at the dark of the moon."

Johanna raised an eyebrow. "Hard on the feet, stumbling around all those rock pools at night."

"Also said to be flavored with the blood of said virgins," Jaufre said, inspired.

"Oh, well, we should definitely buy some, then."

Besides the camels they had eight horses, one and a spare for each of them, and Félicien's donkey. Hari, too, had insisted on a donkey, purchased in Kashgar.

Sheik Mohammed and his son were also traveling west. The sheik told Jaufre they were returning to their home near Talikan, and offered escort, for a price.

He also renewed his offer to buy North Wind. Eventually he and Jaufre concluded terms for their journey that did not include the stallion, and when they emerged from the tent the old sheik further irritated Johanna by patting her cheek and saying approvingly to Jaufre, "Skin as smooth as mare's milk, my friend, and I have never seen such eyes, like the sky at sunrise. You should make your woman wear a veil, lest she tempt mens' thoughts into covetousness."

Jaufre smiled and bent his head without replying, and hoped he was going to survive the night, never mind the journey. Straightening, he saw the sheik's son's eyes drawn irresistibly to Johanna.

The old man was in love with the horse. The young man was in love with its rider. Jaufre squared his shoulders, feeling the reassuring weight of his father's sword against his back. Neither man would achieve his heart's desire on this trip.

They left Kashgar the next morning, since the heat of the day was easing as the year made its way toward fall. Uncle Cheng saw them off, tears unashamedly streaming down his cheeks. Johanna was the last of his family left to him. At the last moment, Johanna, similarly affected, said urgently, "Come with us, uncle!" She burrowed into his arms, her voice muffled against his tunic. "Who knows what wonders we shall find, far in the west! Come see them with us!"

He wiped his tears on his sleeve and patted her back before pushing her back. "I don't deny that it is tempting, Johanna, but I have merchants expecting cargo in Chang'an. Still, who knows? One day, perhaps, I shall follow."

With that Johanna had to be content. She mounted North Wind and kicked him into a gallop to catch up with her friends, where she reined in and stood in her stirrups to turn and look back for the last time. The large man in the sand-colored robes standing outside the great Kashgar gate raised his arms high above his head. She raised both of hers in return and cried out, something inarticulate, encompassing love, and loss, and farewell.

And then she faced west and nudged North Wind into motion again.

The white bulk of the Pamirs stood blunt and proud against the deep blue sky, on their left as they began to climb up. The way was all ridges and valleys and passes. The narrow trail was beaten down by hundreds of years of travelers' feet but no smoother for that. Rocks rattled down from the hills above, evergreen branches scraped their heads, and in places the trail fell abruptly to the bottoms of distant canyons where the way narrowed to a strip of ground barely wide enough for a camel to pass. Jaufre hooked the lead camel to Hari's donkey and let the sure-footed little beast lead the way. Hari walked behind, omming. He never seemed to be out of breath like the rest of them.

"Straight to heaven," Johanna said, panting.

"How long before we get to the top?" Shasha said.

Johanna touched the purse at her waist. "Father says forty days to the plain."

"Forty days!" It was only their third, and the path before them wound ever upward.

The people who lived between the ridges and in the valleys were few and secretive, and seen only in glimpses. They looked to be hunters, as they were dressed in skins. As the travelers soon found, if they did not mount a constant watch the mountain people were also expert thieves. Exhausted as they were at the end of each day, it was an additional hardship, to be always alert for theft.

When they met oncoming travelers, it was a mad, confused crush of swearing men and animals, jostling for place on the trail (no one wanted the outside edge if they were currently traversing a precipice, which they only too often were) and trying to avoid steaming piles of dung excreted by camels and horses and donkeys choosing to exercise their displeasure by the only means possible to them. There were no caravansaries along this stretch of the Road, and campsites were few, small and mean, lacking in fuel and often in water, which caused them to make camp earlier some evenings so that they could send out scouts to find the nearest stream. If another caravan was there before them, they slept between rocks and under trees at the nearly vertical sides of the trail, everyone out of sorts the next day from having spent the entire night trying not to slip down into whatever abyss they were camping next to. Arguments over who had laid claim to what campsite for the evening increased with altitude, and only Firas' calm, authoritative manner averted some outright clashes.

"I'm glad we brought him," Johanna said, when they were first into the next campsite that evening.

"Me, too," Jaufre said.

Johanna looked at Shasha. "Are you glad we brought him, Shasha?"

Shasha said nothing, but the next time her camel was in reach he took a nip at Johanna's knee.

There was none of the camaraderie that had existed on the crossing of the vast, flat plain they had left so far behind them. There was no singing around the campfire in the evening, as there wasn't much of a campfire and no one had any breath to sing with anyway. There was not even the comfort of light, as the twisting trail, the overhanging bluffs and the narrow valleys cut off the most wayward rays of the sun during the day, and hid the stars at night.

"No wonder Yusuf the Levantine charged so much for his olive oil, " Johanna said one afternoon, toiling ever and ever upward. Like Jaufre and Shasha, she had donned her astrakhan coat very soon after they had begun to climb. She sweated beneath it as the trail rose, but if she took it off the sweat froze to her skin.

Félicien blew loudly into a large and filthy handkerchief. "I came by the northern way when I went first to Khuree. It was much easier."

They all wished he hadn't said that.

"We climb to the seat of heaven itself," Hari said, face raised beatifically to the sky.

Firas, like Hari, seemed impervious to heat and cold alike.

Thirty days into their climb, water would not boil, and even if it would you could stick your finger in it and not be burned. Game thinned out and the birds vanished altogether. They subsisted on dried fruit and nuts, and unleavened bread made from grain they carried with them, when they could find enough water to spare from filling their water sacks. They went thirsty before the livestock did.

Johanna kept North Wind behind her on the trail and picketed near them every night. He was better than a muezzin at sounding the call if someone smelling unfamiliar approached their camp, but she noticed that he ate less than he was used to, and drank every bucket of water dry.

They were all drinking as much water as they could find. It never seemed enough. One morning Johanna noticed that the others' voices were beginning to sound high and thin and somehow from a distance, even if they were standing right in front of her. Wu Li had written of this phenomenon in his book, but it was one thing to read of it happening to other people, and another and very disconcerting thing to experience in person.

Then, one day, she looked off the trail and beheld a sheep such as she had never seen before. He was very fat and bore a pair of enormous, curling horns that she recognized as the precursors of bowls she had seen in Kashgar. He baa'ed at her and bounded away, but they saw more and more of them as they climbed higher. That night they dined on fresh meat for the first time since they entered the mountains. Later that evening they also paid an extortionate amount to the herder to whom the sheep had belonged, who appeared, indignant and wrathful, at the very moment they were cracking the last of the bones for the marrow.

"Excellent timing," Jaufre murmured, and Johanna noticed he added a little to the requested sum. He saw her looking and grinned. "I admire professionalism in any endeavor."

And then the next morning Johanna woke to light, or at least more light than she had become accustomed to over the past month. The trail had begun to level out, and the tall evergreens gave reluctant way to dells of greensward, and then to pasture. They were able to ride again, and Jaufre unhitched Hari's donkey from the lead camel and Hari rode once more with his face upturned to the sun.

"Is this heaven, old man?" Jaufre said.

He smiled without opening his eyes. "It is very nearly nirvana itself, young master." proving that even holy men were subject to the ill humors of the trail.

Spirits rose up and down the line of camels, and soon Félicien had his lute out and was singing a bawdy song about a brute of a husband with a beautiful young wife and a handsome young lover, and the old hag down the village who spoiled everyone's fun. He sang it a second time in Mongol and a third time in Persian, and again in Frankish. He was out of breath and his voice didn't reach far but by the end they could hear snatches of chorus coming at them from up and down the line of camels.

Finally there came one evening when they camped at the edge of a fine, blessedly level pastureland that seemed to extend beyond the horizon, the rough trails and mountain ridges and the dark claustrophobia of the encroaching evergreens only a threatening green wall at their back. Tall mountains lined the horizon on every side with sharp, menacing peaks clad in white, but next to their campsite there was a clear lake fed by a bubbling stream, and even the fact that their fires burned small and sullen and threw off no heat whatsoever was not enough to stem the party's returning vitality. They had fresh meat again that night, and were ready when the sheep's owner materialized very nearly right out of the grass at their feet, rending his beard and crying out for redress. He got it, and a mug of lukewarm tea well sweetened with honey to send him on his way rejoicing.

Fatima and Azar joined them at their fire, Azar bringing his tambour and Fatima her finger cymbals. No one was in very good voice but they could gasp out the lyrics. It was sort of like poetry, Shasha said later, if poetry was chanted out to the rhythm of a drum and the clash of cymbals.

The sheik and his son joined them, too, solemn but attentive, light from the diminutive fire casting long shadows on their faces. A waxing moon rose above the horizon. Fatima and Azar disappeared arm in arm, whispering and giggling. Firas sat next to Shasha, dignified and silent, while she mended a large tear in one of Jaufre's tunics by the dim light of the campfire.

The sheik stirred. "Jaufre of Cambaluc, I would renew my offer to buy your horse."

"You do me too much honor, Sheik Mohammed," Jaufre said. "I am desolated to have to repeat my refusal."

From his picket nearby, North Wind whickered.

"Five thousand bezants," the sheik said, which was quite an advance on his last offer, and had the added advantage of being currency they wouldn't have to change when they arrived at last at the shores of the Middle Sea. They could tell by his expression he didn't see how they could refuse it.

Firas bent forward to look around Shasha, courteous and perfectly polite. "I believe you heard the young sir's answer, effendi."

The sheik was silenced, and seemed to sigh. He said something to his son in a low voice none of them caught and rose to his feet. "Then I must bid you goodnight." He sketched a small nod that was almost a bow in their general direction, and strode off. With his elaborate headdress and his sweeping skirts, he always looked like he was leading a parade.

His son paused for a moment, his eyes on Johanna, as happened far too often for Jaufre's taste, and for Shasha's too, for that matter. "You will not reconsider?"

"I cannot, even if I would, sir," Johanna said, patiently for her. "If I sold him to your father I would be cheating him, because North Wind will not stay where I am not."

His dark eyes held hers for a long moment. "It is as you wish," he said, and turned to follow his father.

"It is as it is," Johanna said. "They'll have two foals out of the Wind, why do they keep asking for him as well?"

"Who wouldn't?" Félicien said cheerfully, and got to his feet. "I'm for bed. How long to cross this plateau, Johanna?"

"Twelve days, my father said," Johanna said.

"A quarter the distance, and it's flat," the goliard said with immense satisfaction.

Jaufre was still staring at the place where the sheik had sat. Johanna nudged him. "What is it?"

"I don't like his insistence on buying North Wind," he said, his mouth a hard line.

"He is very persistent," Johanna said, stretching her arms and yawning.

"It's more than that," Jaufre said.

Unexpectedly, Firas said, "I agree with you, young sir. We should keep a close watch on the horse."

Johanna laughed in mid-yawn. "I'd pay good money for a chance to watch someone try to steal North Wind."

She got up. Shasha assembled her mending and rose to her feet. "I, too, am uneasy," she said.

Firas looked at Jaufre. "You take the first watch, and then wake me." Jaufre nodded.

"Thank you both for taking such good care of my horse," Johanna said with a mock bow. "Whether he needs it or not."

# · Fifteen ·

*The Pamir and Terak Pass*

———

After so long toiling up and up and farther up again, the rolling grassland was a positive luxury. The season was well into fall but the weather held and sunny day succeeded sunny day, although the sky seemed oddly leeched of color. There was fodder to spare for the pack and the riding animals, and plenty of water from snow trickling down from the high mountains, which reared up, jagged and forbidding, all around them.

"The roof of the world," Johanna said.

Jaufre, a practical man, stretched his hand up as if to touch it. "It's as if we are traveling beneath a clear dome."

They moved quickly now, all alone on this vast expanse of tall grasses, for it was late for them to be making this journey. They knew they were one good storm away from wading through snow piled as high as a camel's hump, and there was still a steep trail to descend on the other side of the high plain before they reached an altitude where the wind did not bite into one like a sharp knife.

By using every moment of daylight available to them, they made the top of the pass just after dark on the eleventh day, and everyone was too tired to do much more than wash down a handful of dried fruits and nuts and roll themselves into their blankets. They didn't even bother pitching the yurts, sleeping instead beneath that pale, open sky.

Sometime before dawn something woke Jaufre. The camp was silent but for the occasional grunts and groans of the livestock. There was no smell of woodsmoke so he was awake even before the cooks. Wide awake, and fully alert. Tense, even, although he could not immediately identify any reason why.

He raised his head. Johanna, Shasha, Félicien and Hari were all sleeping quietly.

Firas was missing, his bedroll tossed to one side, barely visible in the bleached light only now beginning to illuminate the eastern horizon.

Moving quietly, Jaufre got to his feet. He felt for his father's sword and strapped it to his back. He walked a short distance away to relieve himself, washed his face and hands in a pool of water just beginning to form a skin of ice, and went to check on North Wind. The great white beast was sleeping, strapped in a thick felt blanket. Jaufre felt a smile tug at the corners of his mouth. As tired as she must have been last night, Johanna had still first attended to North Wind. He ran his hand down North Wind's neck, and noticed that the big horse had lost some weight during their journey up and over the Roof of the World. The sooner they got back to sea level and a more civilized speed of travel, the better for them all. Jaufre was looking forward to the baths in Kerman.

There was a whisper of sound and something struck the back of his head very hard. The last thing he heard was an outraged whinny from North Wind.

He woke for the second time that morning from a ferocious headache that seemed to center right in the middle of his forehead. He blinked dazedly at the sky.

"Jaufre?" Shasha's voice was welcome but very loud. He winced.

"Can you sit up?"

He didn't know if he could. Hands tugged at him. Oh well, if he must. He sat up and vomited immediately, although there was very little in his stomach given that he had not broken his fast that morning. "What happened?" he said, blinking. Shasha's face blurred into two Shashas and then one again.

"Can you stand?"

He thought about it while listening to try to see what was going on beyond his currently lamentable range of vision. "If I have help."

She took one arm and someone else took his other arm. He recognized him. Félicien. Good. He was on his feet again. Also good, although his balance seemed to be questioning the vertical in a way it never had before. "Where is Firas?"

"I don't know."

"What's happening?"

"Look."

"What?"

Shasha's voice had never sounded so grim. "Look."

He blinked again. His vision cleared finally. He immediately wished it hadn't.

There was a hand, an arm, a leg, neatly severed from their bodies. He heard cries, cut off abruptly. Hard-faced men with bloodied swords stood in a circle around a group of people. He recognized Fatima's voice. She was screaming out Azar's name.

In the center of the circle Johanna stood alone, facing Gokudo. In one hand he held his naginata. He had Jaufre's father's sword strapped to his back and Johanna's purse now fastened to his belt. "As we agreed," he said to the sheik. "The horse is yours. The girl is mine," He grabbed Johanna's arm.

"No, she is not!" she said, and yanked free.

He grabbed her again and this time she screamed as loudly as she could. "North Wind! To me! North Wind!"

North Wind answered her loudly and there was the sound of trampling hooves and men's curses, but the sheik had evidently enough men to restrain even North Wind.

The sheik's son said, "Father."

The sheik made a motion with his hand. "A bargain is a bargain, my son." His son was silenced. His eyes met Jaufre's.

You die first, Jaufre thought.

Farhad reddened and dropped his eyes.

Gokudo began to drag Johanna away, a mistake, because she got her feet under her and tripped him. He almost fell and she was three steps away and moving fast when he caught her again. She fastened her teeth in his arm, and he gasped involuntarily. His face congested with fury and he hit her, brutally hard, knocking her teeth loose from his arm. She took immediately advantage of her mouth being free again. "North Wind! North Wind! To me!"

There was the sound of hooves striking and a man cried out in pain. This time North Wind sounded enraged. Come on, boy, Jaufre thought. He took a step forward, only to feel something sharp prod his back. He looked around and saw a hard-faced man with a grin on his face, holding a spear.

They were all of them being held at spear point, he realized. Shasha's face was twisted into a snarl and she looked coiled, ready to spring. Félicien was white to his hairline. He couldn't see Fatima or Azar or Malala or Ahmed, although a woman was sobbing somewhere nearby who sounded like Fatima. Hari was sitting on the ground with his legs crossed and his feet on his knees, eyes closed, omming, which Jaufre did not find useful. He heard Gokudo curse and looked around to see that Johanna had tried to trip him again, crying out, "North Wind! North Wind!"

This time Gokudo lifted her off her feet and carried her to his horse, to which a second horse was tethered. He threw Johanna up on the second horse and tied her hands to the pommel and her feet beneath its belly. She immediately kicked it in the belly so that it reared and plunged, the hooves narrowly missing Gokudo.

"Johanna!" Jaufre said. He would have gone to her, nothing would have stopped him, but he was seized from behind with arms like iron. "No, young sir, wait," a voice whispered in his ear. "Wait."

The man with the spear was laying on the ground, his blood spilling from a wide cut on his throat. So, Jaufre realized, were all of their guards. It had happened so fast and so quietly that, incredibly, no one seemed to have noticed what was happening behind them, their attention fixed as it was on the drama playing out in front of them. He looked at Firas, bloody scimitar in his hand, and found himself unable to utter a word.

Firas gave an approving nod and held up his hand, palm out. "Wait, young sir," he said in a low voice. "Wait."

Gokudo seized the reins of Johanna's horse and dragged him down with an iron hand and struck her again. Blood spurted and this time Jaufre could not help himself. "Johanna!"

Gokudo looked around and grinned. "Ah, young Jaufre. How nice that you woke up from your nap in time for me to say goodbye." He looked from Jaufre to Johanna and back again. "A little bruised but she will warm my bed nicely between here and Cambaluc." The grin widened. "You must know that Wu Li's widow has placed no conditions on her return to Everything Under the Heavens, other than that she be breathing."

Jaufre lunged forward and was restrained by hands like iron. Firas again, although Gokudo, flush with his triumph, perhaps also in anticipation of the joys of the night to come, didn't notice who was holding Jaufre back. The crowd had stepped forward over the slain mercenaries and had packed itself densely around Gokudo and Johanna and around Jaufre and Firas, occluding Gokudo's view and hampering his actions. Later Jaufre would realize they had done this deliberately, put themselves at risk out of respect for Wu Li and affection for Wu Li's daughter and foster son.

"Wait, young sir!" Firas' voice said in his ear. "Wait."

"Wait for what?" But something in Firas' voice made him stop struggling.

"Look," Firas said, a hand pointing over Jaufre's shoulder.

Jaufre followed the direction of that pointing finger, past the suddenly still form of the samurai, yet to climb on his horse, past the faces of the sheik and his son who looked as if all at once they felt less in control of the situation, past the hard-faced men with swords who were hastily cleaning them and putting them back in their scabbards, as if to show they had never drawn them in the first place, the various body parts scattered around them to the contrary. Some of them began to melt back into the crown of caravaners, and shortly thereafter was heard the sound of galloping hooves.

"Look, young sir." Firas' voice was quietly insistent. Jaufre looked, and looked again, and then he didn't need Shasha's sharp indrawn breath to tell him his eyes were not deceiving him.

They had thought Uncle Wu Cheng's caravan was large, and so it had been. A thousand camels was a lot of camels, and the people necessary to feed and care for them and to pack them and drive them amounted to a respectably-sized town.

What was coming at them from over the eastern horizon was something else again.

It was a veritable wave of men on horseback, hundreds of them, thousands of them. The black wave filled the horizon from end to end, rank after rank after rank of them, holding their mounts to a disciplined trot, the silver ornaments on their saddles blindingly bright in the rays of the rising sun. As they came closer Jaufre could see that they wore leather coats wrapped and tied with sashes, calf-high leather boots, and helmets with horse-tail plumes. Each carried a bow and a quiver filled with arrows with different heads, and wore knives and swords thrust into their sashes.

On they came, and onward, never breaking stride, and the sound of that many hooves was the sound of approaching thunder. A black banner snapped over a man who rode a little in front of the rest of them.

Gokudo shouted and Jaufre looked around to see that Johanna had pulled her mount free of Gokudo's grip and was galloping toward the oncoming army. She shouted but she was too far away for them to hear her words.

"She has courage, the young miss," Firas said approvingly.

"What is she doing!" Félicien said. "Has she completely lost her mind?"

Shasha looked up at Jaufre. "Do you think—"

"Maybe," he said, his eyes straining to see the features of the leader, coming toward them at what felt at the time like an agonizingly slow trot.

He was so intent on the far prospect that he neglected the near, and jumped a little when Firas appeared in front of him. He had Jaufre's sword in one hand and Johanna's purse in the other. Numbly, Jaufre accepted the sword, and with a bow Firas offered the purse to Shasha, who accepted it with a long look that even Jaufre in this fraught moment could see promised a later reward.

He removed his sword from its worn leather sheath to see if it had come to any harm. It had not, and he slid it home again. No blood stained its blade, and he knew a burning shame that he had been taken prisoner without so much as raising a hand, let alone his sword, in his own or anyone else's defense.

He looked toward Gokudo, expecting to see his body laid out on the ground like the spearmen who had held them hostage but it was impossible to see over the heads of the crowd that had now surged forward.

He looked at Firas and found Shasha binding his arm. "Did you kill him?"

"Not quite," Firas said. "May I suggest, young sir, that you find North Wind and soothe him as much as you are able?" He nodded at the oncoming horde. "We do not want him to discourage any attempts at friendship the young miss might be making."

Johanna was reining in next to the man who appeared to be leading the army on horseback. He halted, and they seemed to be speaking. After a few minutes he pulled the knife from his belt and Jaufre froze, his heart thudding dully in his ears.

The sun flashed on the blade of the knife as it moved in one swift, clean gesture. Johanna's bonds fell and her hands were free. Jaufre breathed again. Johanna turned her horse and kicked it into a trot to match the leader's, and Jaufre went to look for North Wind.

He found the stallion restrained with a rope around his neck and another around each foot. Someone had even managed to loop one around his tail. Not that it had appeared to have helped them restrain the stallion. Two men were laying on the ground, one silent, one moaning in pain. Four men held tightly onto the remaining ropes as if terrified of what would happen if they let them go. They were right to do so, as North Wind's fury was incandescent. His ears flat, his teeth bared, with every plunge he jerked harder on the ropes holding him. As Jaufre came up he yanked one of the four off his feet, although the man scrambled up again immediately and scuttled out of the way of those deadly hooves. He would be free in the next moment and on a rampage that saw no difference between friend and foe.

"North Wind," Jaufre said in a loud voice.

The horse ignored him and plunged again. The end of the rope around his neck was tangled in his forefeet, and he was bleeding from where the ropes had scraped all four hocks. "North Wind," Jaufre said again, and in what was probably the bravest act of his life to date walked steadily forward, a hand raised, palm out. "North Wind," he said in Mandarin, knowing that the words were unimportant, that the tone was all, "North

Wind, Johanna is all right. I will take you to her. North Wind, settle down, settle down now. Calm yourself, calm down, calm down now."

The ears stayed flat and the teeth bared but at least the stallion stopped plunging. Jaufre caught the eyes of the man North Wind had dumped on his back and gave a tiny jerk of his head, still talking to the horse. The man looked as if he might burst into tears of gratitude, and signaled to the other three men to follow his lead. He must have known something about horses in general for he did not just drop the rope, he laid it down slowly, and then backed up one step at a time. He was followed in lock step by the other three, and when they'd reached a safe distance they turned and ran. Wise of them. North Wind never forgot a smell, and when Johanna saw the state of his legs, the men would be in mortal danger from both of them.

Jaufre kept North Wind's attention on him. "North Wind, North Wind, North Wind, that's my boy, that's my good boy, be calm now, be quiet now, North Wind."

One ear came forward. Another. North Wind whickered and stretched out his nose to that familiar voice, and by the grace of the chariot of Arjuna, whose wheels are right effort and whose driver is truth, Jaufre had a bit of sugar in his pocket. He held it out in his left hand, just in case North Wind tried to take it off at the wrist, but the horse dropped his head and nuzzled his palm.

By the time he had calmed North Wind, Johanna came trotting up alongside the Mongol baron. Her hands and feet had been cut free and she had wiped the blood from her face, although bruises were already forming. Evidently her jaw wasn't broken because she was chatting as freely with the baron as she would have with Yusuf the Levantine over a particularly good press of olive oil.

Gokudo was still missing. Those men of Gokudo's still standing had been melting backwards even as the Mongol soldiers approached. The Mongol army took no notice, at least not yet. Everyone else stood stock still, watching Johanna approach at the head of an army with varying degrees of stupefaction.

"Jaufre, Shasha!" Johanna said. "Do you remember Baron Ogodei?"

"I would say I did regardless," Shasha said in a murmur, and raised her voice. "Of course! My lord Ogodei, very well met!"

"Lord Ogodei," Jaufre said, bowing. "It is an honor to meet you again."

"Hah! Not only the honorable Wu Li's daughter, but the honorable Wu Li's adopted son and the honorable Wu Li's adopted sister-in-law." He smiled benignly upon them. "Well met indeed. I had not looked to find such pleasant companionship on the Road this day." His eyes traveled across the assembled company, which now included everyone from the lowliest cook and camel driver to the sheik and his son, immobile in their voluminous white robes. As the baron's eyes fell upon them they seemed to recall themselves and immediately saluted him, touching their right hands to heart, lips and head.

He nodded and dismounted, revealing himself to be Shasha's height but twice as wide. His face was round and flat, his black eyes slanted up at the corners, and his skin was the gold of old coins. He was beardless but for two long mustaches trailing down to his chest, like those of Uncle Cheng. He looked to have spent every one of his thirty years in the saddle, bow and sword in hand, which indeed he had and which in part accounted for his rapid ascension up the ranks of the Mongol army.

Johanna brought her leg over the pommel and slid down into Jaufre's arms. For just a moment she leaned against him, and he thought he felt a fine tremble go through her body, but she straightened at once and went around her horse's head to the baron.

"I claim the Khan's justice, Ogodei of the Mongols."

He seemed to sigh. "Of course, Wu Li's daughter. Make camp," he said to his aide, who seemed a little bemused, probably at his commander taking what amounted to orders from a sixteen-year old girl. And not even a Mongol girl, at that.

Johanna turned to Jaufre, her face sharp with anxiety. "North Wind?"

"He's fine."

She looked around. "Where is Gokudo?" She saw Jaufre's sword. "Did you kill him?"

"Firas fought with him," Jaufre said. "He got my sword and your purse back, but he was wounded. Gokudo got away."

"He can't have gotten very far away," she said fiercely, and whirled back to Ogodei. While they had been talking, his horse had been led away, a yurt had appeared as if by magic, and a carpet had been laid before its entrance. Pillows and more carpets had been piled into a comfortable couch on the carpet, and thereon Ogodei took his seat. Someone hurried up with a tray holding a pitcher and a cup. Ogodei poured the cup full and drank it off. "Now, where is this villain for which you seek the swift and sure justice of the Great Khan, young Johanna?"

Johanna bowed. "He seems to have vanished, lord." Her tone of voice indicated her disbelief that Gokudo had done any such thing.

"Has he." Ogodei's eyes ran over the assembled crowd. "Has he, indeed." He raised his voice. "Who here knows the whereabouts of the Nippon mercenary who so cravenly attacked this caravan?"

"Is there a reward?" someone shouted, and someone else laughed.

Ogodei did not laugh. "There is death," he said mildly, "for anyone who aided his escape."

The caravaners, in a mood to celebrate their own escape from robbery, rape and murder, sobered at his words. Into this silence Fatima pushed forward to Johanna's side, her face tearstained, and said, "I add my demand for the Khan's justice against this man. He killed my affianced husband."

"Fatima!" Johanna cried. "Azar? Dead?"

A cold hand clutched hers. "Do not be kind, Johanna. I could not bear it."

The sheik, silent in the front row of the crowd, stirred and moved forward, in spite of the protests murmured by his son. He arrayed himself before Ogodei and bowed low. "I am the Sheik Mohammed, of Talikan. It may be that I have information useful to you." He waited.

"It may be that you do," Ogodei said, when it became evident the sheik had finished speaking. "I will not know how useful until you tell me what it is."

"It seems to me to be very valuable information," the sheik said.

Ogodei almost smiled, and did shake his head. "You Persians," he said. "You always have to bargain." His eyes narrowed and he leaned forward. "Mongols don't bargain. We take. We take? And you die." He let that sink in for a moment, and then leaned back. "You give? And you live." He waved a negligent hand. "Possibly."

The sheik was as cool as a lake on a calm spring morning, although people near him began sidling away. No one who had ever lived for an hour beneath Mongol rule doubted Ogodei's plain statement was anything other than simple fact.

Ogodei waited without impatience, until the sheik bowed his head, indicating an obeisance to a superior force, and gave a wave of his hand. His son vanished into the crowd, to return some minutes later with Gokudo, bound and under guard.

Johanna stepped forward. "This, lord, is the man who stole my horse and who tried to kidnap me."

Fatima pointed in turn. "This is the man who killed Azar of Kashgar, son of Kalal."

Displaying a fine sense of the dramatic, Firas came up leading North Wind, although the instant North Wind scented Johanna he shouldered Firas to one side and headed straight for her, people moving hastily out of his way. He sniffed her all over once, and then again, just to make sure, after which threw back his head and whinnied a challenge to anyone who thought they could mishandle him so rudely and get away with it. Prudently, no one took him up on it.

"We have traveled these five days almost without stopping," the baron said, still mild. "We will join you here in your camp and refresh ourselves. While we rest," he said, looking at Johanna, "we will attend to the matter brought to our attention by the daughter of the honorable Wu Li." He looked at Gokudo, and though his expression remained amiable Gokudo seemed to shrivel in place. He turned from to Gokudo to the sheik and his son, who looked wary but declined to shrivel. "We will meet in front of my ger to talk of these and other things when the sun is high."

They were dismissed. Two of Ogodei's soldiers sauntered casually over to stand on either side of Gokudo, while four more arranged themselves around the sheik and his son. There was a great bustle as the soldiers made their camp, yurts going up as if by magic, horses fed and picketed, and dried meat and skins of koumiss produced practically out of the air.

Hari was fascinated and walked among them, listening to them talk, now and then asking a question and listening intently to the answer. The soldiers tolerated him, but then Mongols were notoriously easy-going when it came to priests. They had so many gods already, what was one or two more? He ended his tour sitting before Ogodei, who questioned him closely about India, although Hari was more conversant with temples and gods than he was rulers and standing armies.

Johanna accompanied the others back to their campsite, North Wind following close behind. He wasn't ready to let Johanna out of his sight. She received her purse back from Shasha, made appropriate thanks to Firas, and tied it again to her belt. "Are you all right?" she said to Jaufre. "What happened to you? You were gone when the noise woke us. You and Firas both."

He reached a hand up to the back of his head and winced. "Something woke me up. I went to check on North Wind and I think that someone hit me on the head. What happened to you?"

Shasha found her pack and got out a smelly yellow salve that she smeared impartially on Johanna's cheek and Jaufre's crown. "The noise of the fighting woke us up, and then—"

"—and then he came," Johanna said, almost spitting out the words. "And he dared to put hands on North Wind, and then on me!"

North Wind still came first, Jaufre noted without surprise. "We were lucky today."

"Very," Shasha said.

"Very, very lucky," Félicien said, and the strength seemed to go out of his legs and he dropped the bedroll he was folding and slumped down on it all of a heap. "Traveling with you is more exciting than I'd bargained for."

Jaufre and Shasha looked accusingly at Johanna, who waved an airy hand. "Yes, well, at least you can't say it's been boring." She smiled as sunnily as she was capable of with the entire left side of her face stiff and swollen.

"What now?" Jaufre said. He sat down, too, feeling a little shaky himself.

Shasha, Firas and Johanna followed suit, and a brief silence fell as everyone took stock of their current circumstances and tried not to dwell on what might have been. After a bit Félicien went for water, and they built a fire, such as it was, and broke their fast with lukewarm tea, unleavened bread and dried fruit.

"I'd kill for a bowl of noodle soup," Johanna said. "Hot, hot, hot noodle soup."

"Never, ever say that again," Jaufre said. "Or at least not until we get down out of the mountains, where fire burns as it ought." The sun was warm on his back and Shasha had given him a powder in his tea that had eased the ache in his head. "What will Ogodei do, do you think?"

Johanna shrugged. She was putting a good face on it but she was clearly feeling her bruises, and the anger and indignation that had buoyed her thus far was ebbing. She yawned suddenly, her jaws cracking. "He was a friend of Father's."

"But Wu Li is dead," Shasha said.

Johanna nodded. "There are many witnesses to what Gokudo did. At the very least he is guilty of conspiracy, assault, theft. I asked for the justice of the Khan from Ogodei." She shrugged. "Perhaps he will give it. Perhaps he won't." She brightened. "I wonder where he's going. We could ask him for escort."

Shasha shook her head.

"What?"

"Johanna, I doubt very much if one of the generals of a hundred thousand is going to offer the protection of his royal troops to such as us."

"He did for Father."

"Yes, well, and how many camels loaded with Cipangu pearls did we have with us on that trip?"

"We could tell Ogodei everything," Jaufre said.

Shasha was repacking her herbs but her head snapped up at that. "We have no proof."

"By all the round-eyed gods, Shasha. When did Wu Li in his entire life ever fall off of anything with a saddle?"

Johanna, who had been about to doze off, sat bolt upright. "What? What are you talking about?"

Jaufre looked at Shasha, who held his gaze for a long moment before sighing and dropping her eyes. "All right. Tell her."

Jaufre turned to Johanna, squaring up to her as if he were facing an opponent in a duel, which he might very well be. "I checked Wu Li's tack as soon as I could after the accident. His girth was cut through. Not all the way, just enough so that it would snap beneath his weight when he kicked his horse into a run."

The silence that fell over their little campsite was acute and uncomfortable. Félicien and Firas were asleep or pretending to be, and Hari had yet to return from his anthropological expedition into the

Mongol horde. It was just the three of them. It had been just the three of them since Wu Li had died.

"Why didn't you show me the tack?" Johanna said finally. She felt numb, and Jaufre's words were coming to her from a great distance.

"Because it disappeared from the stable right after I looked at it. I asked the stable master and he told me that Gokudo had collected it himself, saying it would be bad luck to keep it and that it must be destroyed."

This time the silence went on longer. Johanna's face was frozen, her eyes dazed, her body, usually a fountain of restless energy, immobile. Jaufre looked at Shasha, who raised a hand slightly as if to say, Wait.

"What else?" Johanna said.

He didn't answer at first, and she said more strongly, "What else did she do, Jaufre? Because there is something else. I can tell just by looking at you."

"I went to Wu Li's room as soon as we heard that he had died," Shasha said. "His eyes were red, and his lips were blue. He was smothered where he lay."

"She killed him," Johanna said.

"Gokudo killed him," Shasha said. "Wu Li was paralyzed only from the waist down. She wouldn't have been strong enough. He fought. There was blood under his fingernails."

"She killed him," Johanna said. "She killed him. Twice. Gokudo was only her tool."

Neither of them contradicted her.

When the sun was high overhead, they gathered again before the big round white ger with the black banner flying from its peak. Ogodei relaxed on his couch, an intricately woven carpet beneath him and a flagon of koumiss in his hand. "Johanna of Cambaluc, daughter of Wu Li, niece of Wu Cheng, you have asked for the Khan's justice."

Johanna rose, tall and proud and white to the lips. "I have, lord."

"Speak."

She kept it short, relating the incidents of the past night in full, pointing to Gokudo and the sheik in turn, ignoring the wounded look in the son's eyes. "He and they are guilty of conspiracy, my lord. They are guilty of assault and murder—three people are dead, including Azar of Kashgar, my dear friend and the betrothed of Fatima, daughter of Ahmed and Malala, also of Kashgar, and also a dear friend."

The baron quaffed koumiss. The smell of the fermented mare's milk was strong enough to reach Johanna's nostrils, and she repressed a sudden wave of nausea. She knew what she was asking for was just. She would not shame her father by asking for less than what was due his memory. "A dozen are wounded, some severely, and one woman was raped. I have no doubt more would have been had you not come upon us."

"Let us adhere to the facts of the matter, Wu Li's daughter." Ogodei said, pleasant as always. "If we venture into speculation we will be here until the snow falls."

Johanna bent her head. "It is my joy always to obey you, my lord." It was not merely an empty saying. When Johanna bent her head to Ogodei, she bent it to the power of the Khan in Cambaluc. "He conspired with the Sheik Mohammed to kidnap me and to steal my horse. We all heard him say so." She looked around and heads nodded vigorously in confirmation. "He assaulted me." She pointed at her face. "He announced his intention of doing more than that on the Road to Cambaluc." More nods. Gokudo had a fine, penetrating voice. Everyone had heard him clearly.

"Well," Ogodei said. "He is, clearly, guilty of all of these things, and of stupidity as well, since he did all these things and then convicted himself of them out of his own mouth." He drank koumiss and looked at Johanna. "What is the penalty he must pay, Wu Li's daughter?"

"His life," Wu Li's daughter said.

Gokudo made a sudden movement, and subsided when the Mongol soldiers at his sides reminded him they were there.

The baron raised his eyebrows. "You are not dead, Wu Li's daughter."

"Others are," Johanna said.

"You are not even much hurt."

"Others are."

"Your horse has been returned to you—he is very like a horse I bet on last winter in Cambaluc, did you know? A horse owned and raced by Edyk the Portuguese. Perhaps he is of the same lineage?"

"Perhaps," Johanna said through stiff lips. It was a warning, and kindly meant, but she could not stop, not now that she knew the whole story. "There is also the matter of blood guilt, lord."

Gokudo, unable to speak behind his gag, slumped a little between his guards.

The baron raised his eyebrows. "What blood guilt is this?"

"As I told you, Gokudo is a member of my father's household."

"Johanna—" Shasha said.

"He came there as bodyguard to my father's second wife."

The baron nodded. "Yes, I recall. The honorable Dai Fang."

"Not so honorable, my lord. She dishonored my father with Gokudo."

Gokudo came alive again, struggling and trying to shout from behind his gag.

This time the baron's eyebrows ascended all the way to his hairline. "You have proof of this?"

"The word of my foster brother and my aunt, and myself."

"Very well."

"By the observations of my foster brother, Jaufre of Cambaluc, my father's saddle was tampered with so that he would fall from his horse that day."

The baron looked at Jaufre, who nodded. The baron said, "But Wu Li lived beyond his accident, did he not?"

"He did, my lord. Too long, as it happened, because Gokudo and Dai Fang grew impatient, and smothered him in his bed."

Gokudo had managed to work his gag free. "Bitch! No one will believe your whore's words!"

"As attested to by my aunt," Johanna said steadily.

The baron looked at Shasha, who nodded in turn.

A murmur ran through the crowd, soldiers and merchants alike. Wu Li was well known to the Road, and those who traveled thereon. The baron suppressed a sigh. "So it is death you ask for, Wu Li's daughter?"

"It is death I am owed," she said. "And not just any death."

"Oh god, Johanna, no," Jaufre said beneath his breath. Next to him Shasha closed her eyes and shook her head. Félicien looked at Firas, whose countenance was more than ordinarily mask-like.

"Give him the death of the carpet, lord," Johanna said clearly, raising her voice so that it could be heard.

There was an immediate tumult, not least of which came from Gokudo, who called her names until at a gesture from the baron one of his guards gagged him again.

The baron in turn rose to his feet. "It shall be so," he said, and the crowd, pausing only long enough to hear the words, shouted their approval, over and over again.

There wasn't a great deal of ceremony to it, and no waiting period. Gokudo was hustled to a flat space beyond the camp. Mongol soldiers mounted their horses and formed two lines with a clear lane between. A carpet was brought, the very carpet that had supported the baron's couch. Gokudo, cursing and struggling, was swallowed up by Mongol soldiers and when they saw him again he was rolled into the carpet. All they could see of him was a topknot of black hair.

The carpet was laid between the two rows of horses. The baron stood at one end and raised his arm. Another company of soldiers waited at the other end of the lane. When the baron's arm fell, they kicked their horses into a gallop. They thundered down the lane and over the rolled carpet. The noise was so loud from the crowd and the soldiers that nothing could be heard from inside the carpet, although Jaufre would have sworn he heard the man scream.

The baron's arm raised and fell again, and again the company of horses thundered down the lane and over the carpet. Again, the arm fell, and again the horses galloped, and again, and again. Red began to seep through the carpet, and they paused to unroll it to see if Gokudo was dead. He was unrecognizable by now, a mess of blood and splintered bone wrapped in a mass of quilted black cloth, but unbelievably the blood pulsing from many wounds indicated that he was indeed still alive.

Ogodei shouted something and his soldiers cheered and banged their bows against their shields. Two held open Gokudo's mouth and a third rammed it full of horse manure, of which there was by now a plentiful supply. The broken body jerked in a horrible, boneless struggle. They rolled him back into the carpet and thundered the horses over him another three times.

This time when they unrolled the carpet he was definitely dead.

The baron beckoned to Johanna, and she marched toward him on stiff legs, her back very straight, her chin very high, her face like stone. She wanted to spit on Gokudo's remains, but she could not bring herself even to look at him, and her mouth was too dry for spitting anyway. "Lord?"

"Is your call for justice satisfied, Wu Li's daughter?"

"I have received the justice of the Khan," Johanna said steadily, "and I am satisfied."

"And the sheik and his son, Wu Li's daughter? The samurai's co-conspirators? They have also gravely offended you. What to them?"

"I leave them to your good judgement, my lord," Johanna said. "So far as I know they are only thieves."

The expression on the sheik's face indicated that he did not view her words as a compliment, but he said nothing, and he stopped his son from speaking as well. He'd had dealings with Mongols before this, and he knew how little the Mongols wished for trouble with the Persians. They had other fish to fry.

"Thievery," Ogodei said pensively. "For a first offense, that usually means the sacrifice of the right hand."

Johanna swallowed hard, and repeated, "I leave their punishment to your good judgement, lord."

The baron approached her and bent his head so that his lips were next to her ears. "Did no one warn you, Wu Li's daughter, that vengeance can be as bitter on the tongue as it is sweet?"

By unspoken agreement Johanna and her party took their leave of the rest of the caravan, packing and riding away from that place of horror as quickly as they could. As they were leaving camp Fatima ran up. "Johanna!" She reached up and clasped Johanna's hand between her own and looked deeply into her eyes. "Thank you," she said.

Tears stung Johanna's eyes. "I'm so sorry about Azar," she said.

"He is avenged," Fatima said simply, and ran back to her parents.

The trailhead down was reached in less than an hour and Johanna was grateful that it was another narrow trail, so that they would have to go single file and she didn't have to talk to anyone. She had to stop once to vomit, and Shasha, who was behind her, said nothing.

Johanna wiped her mouth. "You should have told me."

"Before we left Cambaluc, do you mean? And what would you have done? Killed Gokudo? Killed Dai Fang? Tell, me, Johanna, would we now be a thousand leagues from Cambaluc if you had done so? Or would we be locked in the same dungeon your grandmother died in?"

"You should have told me," Johanna said fiercely. "I am no longer a child, Shasha. You are no longer allowed to protect me from harsh realities of our lives."

Shasha threw up her hands in disgust and climbed back on her horse. Johanna grabbed a handful of North Wind's mane and threw a leg over his broad back, and they moved rapidly down the trail without another word.

That night they made a cold camp beneath the evergreen trees that had reappeared along the trail. No one spoke very much or slept very well.

At noon the next day the sheik and his men materialized out of the forest, surrounding them.

Johanna, too tired to be afraid, said, "Sheik, you are beginning to annoy me."

"He let you go," Shasha said. "Ogodei just—let you go?"

Félicien looked frightened and clung tight to his donkey. Hari said in a sterner voice than any of them had heard before, "Your god is named Allah, is he not? Would he approve, I wonder, of your attacking and robbing innocent travelers on the road?"

Firas said nothing and did nothing, sitting immobile on his mount.

The sheik ignored them both. "I will take the horse now."

Johanna laughed, an edge of hysteria to her voice. "Have you learned nothing, sheik? He will not go with you!"

"And I will take the woman as well," the sheik said, "since the horse will not go anywhere without her."

"No, you will not!" Jaufre said, reaching for his sword.

"I am sorry," Farhad said from beside him, and drove his sword into Jaufre's back.

He heard Johanna scream. Heard Shasha cry out. Heard Félicien say, "No no no no no!" Heard Hari om.

Felt himself falling.

Twice in two days, he thought.

Johanna, he thought.

And then the black rose up to engulf him and he thought no more.

# · Sixteen ·

——

"**Y**ou are a samurai, are you not?" the baron said. "More specifically, a ronin, I believe it is called? A samurai who answers to no lord?" Gokudo, bound hand and foot but demonstrably alive, gave a curt nod. His topknot was missing, as was his quilted armor, leaving him dressed in trousers and a simple tunic.

"I thought so," the baron said. "We tried invading Cipangu. Twice. You defeated us, both times." He smiled. "It takes a great warrior to defeat a Mongol army."

Gokudo, who had been shown the body of the hapless soldier who had been substituted for his own, said through dry lips, "Thank you, my lord."

"Yes," the baron said, "indeed, you owe me gratitude for your life. Such a bloodthirsty child she is, the daughter of the honorable Wu Li."

Gokudo spat out a hate-filled curse and called the ancestry of Wu Li's daughter into serious question.

The baron strolled forward and leaned down to say in Gokudo's ear. "The honorable Wu Li of Cambaluc was my very good friend." He stood straight again and kicked Gokudo once, very hard, between his legs. The guards standing around the inside of the ger laughed heartily.

Gokudo's mouth opened in a silent scream and he doubled up on the baron's carpet, scrubbed not entirely clean of blood.

"That is the last time you will insult him in my presence," the baron said pleasantly, "is that understood?"

Gokudo managed a nod.

"Good. I have no doubt his daughter was perfectly right. Such righteous wrath! She was a torch lit from within. If she were anyone else's daughter..." He looked down at Gokudo again. "No, you killed him, that much is certain, and your life is forfeit thereby. So is the so honorable Dai Fang's, if it comes to that. I shall have to see what I can do about that when next I return to Cambaluc."

The baron sighed. "There is an ineradicable stain on my own character for sparing you, and for sparing the Sheik Mohammed, who conspired with you, and indeed for sacrificing of one of my own men in your place."

It did not appear as if that stain weighed heavily upon him.

"However." The baron's flagon had been refilled and he drank deep. He looked again at the bound man trying not to choke on his own vomit on the floor of the baron's ger. "It may be that I have a use for you."

"I cannot return to Cipangu, lord," Gokudo said, gasping for breath. "I will be slaughtered by my enemies the instant I step foot on shore."

Ogodei waved this comment away as inconsequential. "You have skills I believe I will find useful in many places," he said. "Come, get up."

A nod and Gokudo's hands and feet were free and he was assisted roughly to his feet, where he stood, swaying. "Thank you, lord," he said, bowing as deeply as he was able without falling over.

Ogodei nodded, accepting fear and deference as his just due, and smiled. "You are ronin no more," he said.

"No, my lord," Gokudo said.

# ACKNOWLEDGMENTS

My profound gratitude to Michael Cattagio, reference librarian, retired (not so much). No one has ever been quicker on the draw when I ask for information I need right now.

Thanks also go to freelance editor Laura Anne Gilman, who coped womanfully with a manuscript delayed when I fell off a ladder in my garage and sprained my wrist so badly I couldn't type for three weeks. That will interfere with the story going forward. I can't believe I made my deadline. I wouldn't have but for Laura Anne's willingness to work nights and weekends. She also brags on Twitter (@LAGilman) when she gets to read a new Stabenow book before anyone else.

You know when an author realizes she has reached the ne plus ultra of her profession? When she discovers a cartographer among her fans. Dr. Cherie Northon (and I bet Thom had a hand in it, too), take a bow for the terrific map.

And didya see that magnificent cover art? Gere Donovan Press, people. S'all I'm sayin'.

# Glossary

**Balasaga** An historical province of Iran.

**Bao** A personal seal. Chinese.

**Beda** Bedouin.

The Silk and Song **Bureau of Weights and Measures** No two nations back in 1322 measured anything the same way, so here for the sake of narrative clarity and my sanity time is measured in minutes, hours, days, weeks, months and years, and no notice is taken of that error in Julius Caesar's 45 BC calendar that wouldn't be corrected until 1582 by Pope Gregory XIII.

Travel is measured in **leagues**, about three miles or the distance a man could walk in an hour. Fabric is measured in **ells** from China to England. Smaller lengths are fingers (three-quarters of an inch) and hands (three to four inches).

Google "weights in the Middle Ages" and you get over 8 million hits. Here, I use drams, gills, cups, pints, quarts and gallons in ascending order of liquid measurement. Pounds then ranged from 300 grams to 508 grams, so the hell with it, here it's sixteen ounces (about 453 grams). A hundredweight is a hundred pounds.

**Calicut** Now Kozhikode, India.

**Cambaluc** Built by Kublai Khan. What became the basis for what is now the Forbidden City in Beijing, China.

**Chang'an** Now Xi'an, China.

**Cheche** Pronounced "shesh." A long scarf, usually indigo-dyed blue, worn by Tuaregs. It can be knotted many different ways to keep the sun out of the eyes and protect the neck and face from sunburn. The indigo leeched onto the face and hands of the wearer. Or, alternatively, depending on which story you believe, Tuaregs deliberately dyed their face and hands blue to protect themselves from the sun. I heard both in Morocco.

**Cipangu** Now Japan.

**Currency** Tael: China. Bezants: Byzantium. Drachma: Arabic. Florence: Florins. Venice: Accommodate all currencies but rely on gemstones.

**Ell** The distance from a man's elbow to the tip of his middle finger, or about 18 inches. A standard unit of measurement for textiles in the Middle Ages, and never mind the differences between Scots, English, Flemish, Polish, German and French ells.

**Gujarat** Now a province in northwest India.

**Ibn Battuta** Berber slave trader, 1304–1369, known for writing The Rihla ("The Journey,") an account of his extensive travels throughout the medieval world. Purely for the convenience of my plot, I have advanced his first visit to Kabul by five years.

**Kabul** Now the capital of Afghanistan.

**Khuree** The summer capital of the Mongols. Now Ulan Bator, Mongolia.

**Kinsai** Now Hangzhou, or Hangchow, China.

**Lanchow** Now Lanzhou, China.

**League** The distance one person could walk in an hour. Also defined as about three miles. I have rounded up and down. The Khan's yambs were built every 25 miles, therefore in Silk and Song every eight leagues. The Khan's imperial mailmen rode 200 miles daily, hence sixty leagues. Close enough for government work and fiction.

**The Levant** From Wikipedia: "A geographic and cultural region consisting of the eastern Mediterranean between Anatolia and Egypt… The Levant consists today of Lebanon, Syria, Jordan, Israel, Palestine, Cyprus and parts of southern Turkey. Iraq and the Sinai Peninsula are also sometimes included."

**Middle Sea** The Mediterranean, also known as the Western Sea.

**Mien** Now Myanmar, or Burma.

**Mintan** A short-waisted, long-sleeved coat. Ottoman.

**Mongols and torture**. Yes, they did those things. Those exact things. And more.

**Mysore** Then as now, a city in northwest India.

**Paiza** The royal Mongol passport. The Mongols called it a gerrega.

**Sarik** A headscarf. Ottoman.

**Shang-tu** The summer capital of the Mongols. Now Ulan Bator, Mongolia. Also called **Khuree**.

**Shensi** Now Shaanxi, China.

**Silk Road** A term that did not come into common usage until the twentieth century. Here I use the more generic Road.

**Time** See **Bureau of Weights and Measures** above. In Europe: divided into times for prayer. Matins: midnight. Lauds: 3am. Prime: Sunrise. Terce: Midmorning. Sext: Noon. None: Midafternoon. Vespers: Sunset. Compline: Bedtime.

**Turgesh** Turkey, or Turkish.

**Zeilan** On what is now the Somali-Ethiopian border.

# Bibliography

My intent as a storyteller is always to entertain, but this book also required a great deal of research over many years, and was influenced by the work of many scholars, without whose heavy lifting this by comparison light-hearted romp would not have been possible. Here's a list of just a few of the books that helped Johanna and Jaufre on their way.

Bergreen, Laurence. *Marco Polo, From Venice to Xanadu.*

Bonavia, Judy. *The Silk Road.*

Boorstin, Daniel J. *The Discoverers: A History of Man's Search to Know His World and Himself.*

Burman, Edward. *The Assassins.*

Burman, Edward. *The World before Columbus, 1100–1492.*

Cahill, Thomas. *Mysteries of the Middle Ages: The Rise of Feminism, Science and Art from the Cults of Catholic Europe.*

Collis, Louise. *Memoirs of a Medieval Woman: the Life and Times of Margery Kempe.*

Croutier, Alev Lytle. *Harem, The World Behind the Veil.*

Dalrymple, William. *In Xanadu.*

Dougherty, Martin. *Weapons & Fighting Techniques of the Medieval Warrior.*

Foltz, Richard C. *Religions of the Silk Road.*

Freeman, Margaret B. *Herbs for the Medieval Household for Cooking, Healing and Divers Uses.*

Garfield, Simon. *On the Map, A Mind-Expanding Exploration of the Way the World Looks.*

Gillman, Ian, and Hans-Joachim Klimkett. *Christians in Asia before 1500.*

Grotenhuis, Elizabeth Ten, editor. *Along the Silk Road.*

Hansen, Valerie. *Silk Road, A New History.*

Herrin, Judith. *Byzantium: The Surprising Life of a Medieval Empire.*

Johnson, Steven. *The Ghost Map.*

Lacey, Robert & Danny Danzier. *The Year 1000, What Life Was Like at the Turn of the First Millennium.*

Manchester, William. *A World Lit Only by Fire.*

Newman, Sharan. *The Real History Behind the Templars.*

Ohler, Norbert. *The Medieval Traveller.*

Polo, Marco. *The Adventures of Marco Polo.* Many editions.

Rowling, Marjorie. *Everyday Life of Medieval Travellers.*

Tooley, Ronald Vere. *Maps and Map-Makers.*

Tuchman, Barbara. *A Distant Mirror: The Calamitous 14th Century.*

Turner, Jack. *Spice: The History of a Temptation.*

Weatherford, Jack. *Genghis Khan and the Making of the Modern World.*

Whitfield, Susan. *Life Along the Silk Road.*

Wood, Frances. *The Silk Road, Two Thousand Years in the Heart of Asia.*

# To Be Continued...

Silk and Song will continue in

*By the Shores of the Middle Sea*

Available Fall 2014

⊢——⊣

This book was designed by Jerrod Philipps. It was edited and set by Gere Donovan Press in Portland, Ore. and printed by CreateSpace in the USA.

The text face is Minion Pro, designed by Robert Slimbach. An enlargement and revision of Slimbach's original Minion type (Adobe,1989), it was inspired by the elegant faces of the late Renaissance.

The cover and interior title are set in Neris, designed by Eimantas Paškonis. It takes its name from the river Neris that flows through the designer's hometown of Vilnius, Lithuania.

⊢——⊣

CPSIA information can be obtained at www.ICGtesting.com
Printed in the USA
LVOW12s1546071114

412556LV00006B/778/P